B.G. 4

''Surely, that was part of the plan.''

Adam's voice sharpened. ''Don't pretend you're surprised that I kissed you.''

''If you think I deliberately—'' Petra broke off, too angry for words. Stepping back, she lifted one arm, savoring the prospect of feeling her hand connect with that bitter, brooding face. He neatly deflected her blow.

''Well, get this Mr. Herrald,'' she snapped. ''I have no plans to seduce you, strange as it might seem to you. Nor am I a naive country girl ready to succumb to your macho attentions. I don't want them. Is that clear? It ought to be. But it seems you're the kind of man who thinks he's irresistible.''

Kate Kingston was born in Yorkshire. She is married, has one daughter and two grandchildren and now lives in the Nottingham area—famous for Sherwood Forest! Her interests include walking, embroidery and travel. The idea of writing always beckoned, but Kate feels that it was her meeting with a perfect stranger who predicted that one day she would be a writer, that fired her with the enthusiasm to actually go out and do it.

Books by Kate Kingston

HARLEQUIN ROMANCE

14—BITTER INHERITANCE

Harlequin Books

TORONTO • NEW YORK • LONDON
AMSTERDAM • PARIS • SYDNEY • HAMBURG
STOCKHOLM • ATHENS • TOKYO • MILAN

Original hardcover edition published in 1988
by Mills & Boon Limited

ISBN 0-373-02981-0

Harlequin Romance first edition May 1989

Printed in U.S.A.

CHAPTER ONE

PETRA hadn't expected that Adam Herrald would be quite so tall. In her flat red espadrilles she stood five feet eight inches, but even so she had to tilt her head back to look into his face. And she found herself gazing into a pair of narrowed dark eyes so profoundly bleak that, despite the golden June afternoon, a chill of foreboding touched her. It seemed incongruous against the colourful, lively backdrop of the Dieppe waterfront.

'Miss Macey, of course.' His well-defined lips barely moved, but the deep tones had a flinty quality.

Petra's smile faltered as she took the brown hand held out to her. It was firm and hard, a no-nonsense hand, and somehow it conveyed instant rejection. 'And you must be Mr Herrald,' she murmured.

He nodded. 'I trust you had a pleasant crossing,' he said, with the air of dispensing with the tedious preliminaries.

'We did, thank you.' Petra's words came out a little breathlessly. 'The children seemed to enjoy it.'

She looked down at them; eight-year old Sarah had managed to remain clean, and her shiny ponytail swung neatly on her shoulders. But Patrick had somehow accumulated a distinct grubbiness during the cross-channel voyage. As for herself . . . She glanced ruefully down. Her scarlet cotton trousers were creased and slightly soiled from Thomas's frequent clamberings on to her lap, and her loose white sweater bore a faint coffee stain, marking the moment when Patrick had swung his telescope to peer with all the enthusiasm of an eleven-year-old at a distant tanker. Hers was hardly the kind of appearance she'd wanted to present to anyone, let alone this aloof stranger accustomed to photographing top fashion models and society beauties.

Still, it couldn't be helped. Accompanying three children from England to France was bound to leave its mark, she thought philosophically. And during the journey her only concern had been for them, particularly for Sarah who, it seemed, was prone to sea-sickness.

'I've parked around the corner,' Adam Herrald said. 'Shall we go?'

With a lithe economy of movement he hefted four of the bags and strode ahead. Petra followed at a small distance, for the children seemed to have a great deal to tell their uncle—their *favourite* uncle, Sarah had told Petra earlier.

She stifled a sigh. Until this moment she'd been enjoying the first few hours of this temporary job. She'd felt light-hearted, even happy, at the prospect of three or four weeks in France, away from Casterleigh and the little shop. And Marcus, an inner voice added; especially Marcus, who didn't seem able to come to terms with their broken engagement.

Her thoughts slid away as she fixed her eyes on Thomas's bobbing brown head as he hopped along, one hand clutching the hem of Adam's light sweater. And mentally she shook herself. She'd taken this job to get away, to give herself a breathing space before deciding on her future. And she would *not* keep dwelling on the past three weeks, replaying them like some unsatisfactory tape. Marcus Overton and his mother and Cranbrook Place were behind her now. For the next few weeks she'd wipe that tape and, instead, concentrate on this job which offered a refuge, if only temporarily.

She frowned. A three-day journey to the South of France lay ahead, and she could only hope that Adam Herrald would improve upon further acquaintance.

He'd stopped by a white motor caravan and was unlocking the doors. As Petra reached him he said, 'I've booked rooms for us at a small *auberge* about sixty miles south. And thank you, Miss Macey,' he went on curtly, dismissing Petra's attempts to help him load the luggage, 'but I can manage.'

He turned and looked at her then, a long, cool, assessing stare from eyes no longer bleak, but coldly disparaging. 'Perhaps you'll sit in the back,' he went on. 'You can keep an eye on Thomas. You too, Sarah. And you, Patrick, up in the front beside me. Think you can navigate?' His expression softened, acknowledging the bond between himself and his nephew.

'Of course.' Patrick turned to give Sarah a triumphant glance which Adam interpreted.

'Don't look so smug,' he said lightly. 'You and Sarah will take turns up front. A bit of map-reading won't come amiss for either of you, and it'll keep the peace.'

As they drove along the esplanade Petra stared out of the window. The sea stretched like a broad, turquoise ribbon near the beach, and further out a clear, azure blue reflected the sky. Thomas knelt beside her on the bench-seat, straining to see if the anglers who'd set up their rods on the stones were having any success. The other two children chatted animatedly, bringing their uncle up to date with their news. He put in an occasional word or question, drawing forth more confidences.

Petra listened idly. It was obvious to her that a strong bond of affection existed between them and their uncle. An unlikely alliance on the face of it, she thought, studying the brown nape beneath the thick, glossy hair, and thinking of his features. He had a hard face, the bone structure seeming to have been honed and buffed by experience into a smooth strength over which his olive skin gleamed with a dull warmth. It was a face which gave little away, she thought. And yet there brooded behind the dark, hostile eyes and long, sensuous mouth a suggestion of pain and the courage to endure it.

She sat up sharply, giving all her attention to Thomas, until Sarah began to point out the fittings of the motor caravan. 'If you lift that flap there's a sink and a cooker below. And a fridge, look, Petra. There's even a toilet compartment at the back with a shower and everything.'

'You have quite a little life-support capsule here, Mr Herrald,' Petra smiled, determined to make an effort to chip away the stone of his reserve.

'That,' he said, changing gear smoothly, 'is the general idea of a camper vehicle, Miss Macey.'

His thinly veiled rebuff lit a tiny spark of irritation in Petra, but resolutely she stifled it. The children's holiday must not be blighted by a hostile atmosphere, she resolved. Even so, she itched to make some polite but incisive remark that would cut Adam Herrald down to size.

Thomas's warm little hand slid into hers, and she squeezed it gently. At four years old it was his first time away from his mother, who'd had to go into hospital, and up to now he had been very brave about it. Presently Petra felt the weight of his head against her arm, and she looked down at the fan of dark lashes, the bud of his mouth wrapped around the thumb tip. Moved by his utter trust in her, impulsively she bent and dropped a kiss on the silky head. Then, straightening, she met Adam's gaze reflected in the driving mirror, fixed on her with an expression of acute distaste.

Her face grew hot but she returned his gaze steadily, her eyes a cool and challenging hazel. Perhaps he thought she was putting on an act for his benefit. Trying to ingratiate herself. He could think again, she told herself derisively, her dislike heightened by his expression. He simply wasn't worth the effort of pretence!

She turned back to the window, staring out at the spotted cows grazing in the meadowland. But her sense of misgiving had increased. For some reason, Adam Herrald had taken an instant dislike to her. And perhaps, she reflected, if she'd been given the opportunity of meeting him in London at the interview, his attitude would have told her that this wasn't the job for her.

The post had been advertised in one of the daily newspapers, and in answer to her letter she'd been asked to go up to London to be interviewed by a Mr Stansfield, solicitor and family friend of the Herralds. He had seemed to have no reservations about engaging her. And she, grateful to find a position which offered a temporary escape from her problems, hadn't thought to ask about the man with whom she and the children would be travelling.

But it looked as if Adam Herrald had *every* reservation; he hadn't even bothered to conceal his feelings under a veneer of politeness. He made her feel as if she were an unwelcome irritant—like a thorn or splinter under the skin.

Well, at least she knew where she stood, Petra thought wryly.

She was relieved when, after a couple of hours, they turned in to a gravelled drive between tall iron gates. The Lion d'Or lay beyond—a long, rambling building, creeper-hung and flanked by a profusion of geraniums blazing from urns placed along a terrace that ran the length of the building. On a small lawn at the side Petra could see several white chairs and tables grouped invitingly. A faint breeze fingered the fringes of the bright umbrellas.

The accommodation had been efficiently arranged. Patrick was to share Adam's room; while Petra, Sarah and Thomas were shown up a further flight of stairs to a sprawling attic papered in flowery stripes. After attending to the two children's needs Petra washed and changed, before taking them down to join their uncle and Patrick on the lawn.

They found Adam alone, sitting at one of the white tables and reading a newspaper which he folded and laid aside as he rose. Patrick, he told them, had gone exploring as usual. 'No doubt he'll be back immediately he hears the rattle of crockery,' he added, with a grin for Thomas. 'I've ordered tea.'

His eyes glanced briefly off Petra, as if she were some uninteresting part of the scenery. Yet, unaccountably, she had the feeling that in that casual scrutiny he'd noticed everything—from the honey-tanned skin of her face and arms down to the coral-tipped toes that peeped from her green sandals.

During the light meal he seemed preoccupied, but Patrick talked volubly about the angora rabbits in the orchard behind the hotel, and after the children had hurriedly finished their strawberry tarts they made their excuses and disappeared, leaving Petra alone with Adam.

With the children gone the atmosphere seemed to darken, becoming charged with a curious static as if a storm crackled somewhere close by. Petra broke the ominous hush by lifting the teapot, determined to reduce the tension to an atmosphere of neutrality, if nothing better. 'More tea?' she smiled.

'Not for me, thank you.' The words were courteous, but his tone held a chill as he studied her again, then glanced away sharply.

She put the teapot down. 'Please do go on—reading . . . I mean, I don't want to——'

'Miss Macey,' he broke in abruptly, 'shall we bypass the social niceties and have some straight talking?' Petra started, her eyebrows arching in surprise at his tone, and he went on tersely, 'This is my first opportunity to speak to you alone, so perhaps you wouldn't mind answering a question or two?' His mouth was set and serious, but his face seemed closed and expressionless.

Petra gave back his stare steadily. 'Certainly,' she murmured. 'Naturally it's my duty to satisfy any curiosity you may have about me.'

If he heard the irony in her tone he ignored it. 'I *am* curious,' he said curtly. 'Not so much about *you*, Miss Macey, as about the reason you applied for this particular post. After all, you hardly look the *type* to find much satisfaction in such a—shall we say—domestic situation?' His sombre eyes flicked from the short, pale hair, over the olive-green linen dress—the kind of classic dress which Marcus had liked her to wear, but which she had now spiced up with coral beads and matching belt—to the fragile sandals. And again she had the sensation that he had missed nothing, not even the tiny mole at the base of her throat, nor the white mark left by her engagement ring, fading now but still slightly discernible.

But if her travel-stained appearance earlier had irritated him, it seemed that he found her present bandbox fastidiousness equally unpleasing. She felt a sudden flash of impatience. Why should she care? If he had some hang-up about tall blondes with short, *retroussé* noses, or coral nail varnish or—or *anything*, well, that was *his* problem. She forced herself to return his black gaze with clear, untroubled eyes. 'I hadn't realised that there *was* a recognisable *type* for this kind of job, Mr Herrald,' she said smoothly. 'Certainly the advertisement didn't specify that as one of the requirements.'

She felt her dislike for him harden as momentarily his eyebrows flew together in a black, forbidding bar. The movement shifted the planes of his face for a second, throwing the high, smooth cheekbones into greater relief, and emphasising the structure of his jaw, the deep cleft in his chin. She could only guess at the control usually imposed upon that strong face, and she felt a fleeting pleasure in having succeeded in penetrating his armour, if only briefly.

But his face was bland again as he said shortly, 'As you are aware, my solicitor took care of the advertisement. And I think you're sufficiently intelligent to know what I'm getting at, Miss Macey. And by the way, just how long have you known him? My solicitor, that is, Jack Stansfield?'

His question was totally unexpected. It seemed irrelevant and threw her for a moment. 'Why . . . I met him for the first time when he interviewed me,' Petra said wonderingly.

'Really?' For a moment Adam Herrald was silent.

He doesn't believe me, she thought. But why on

earth not?

Then, running impatient fingers through his hair, he regarded her through thick, black lashes and said coldly, 'You don't look at all like the universal nanny figure, if I might say so. So perhaps you won't mind telling me what you did before you took on this job?'

For a moment Petra's eyes showed an equal frost. 'I'm sorry that my appearance isn't to your liking,' she said very quietly. 'Mr Stansfield seemed perfectly satisfied with my—credentials. And so did your sister, Unity—the children's mother,' she went on with pointed emphasis. 'I spent a couple of hours with her and the children at the hospital last night.'

Adam Herrald made an impatient gesture with his brown, capable hands. 'I know that. Unity rang me and told me a little. But she omitted to mention that . . .' He stopped abruptly. 'And the line was bad. But never mind all that,' he went on, a bite of impatience creeping into his voice. 'Suppose *you* fill in a few details. I've been in Paris for the last three weeks, working to a deadline. Otherwise *I'd* have taken care of the interview,' he added meaningly.

Yes, and you'd have given me one look, Petra finished silently, and told me that the post was filled. And I'll probably never know the reason why. Not that I care particularly, though I doubt *you'd* believe that!

'Well? You've got nothing to hide, have you? And as we'll be thrown into each other's company during this journey—and that will take three days or so—then we might as well get the preliminaries over and done with.'

'I've no intention of corrupting the children, if that's what you're suggesting,' Petra began hotly.

Then she closed her mouth resolutely. Her common sense told her that there was absolutely nothing to be gained by letting this infuriatingly attractive man rattle her. The trouble with him, she told herself crossly, is that just because he's a big noise in the photographic world he thinks he can get away with this high-handed attitude towards lesser mortals. 'To answer your question,' she resumed woodenly a moment later, 'before I took on this job I was a partner with a friend. We had a gift shop in Casterleigh. I sold out my share just over two months ago.'

In that one respect, she reflected sadly, she'd conformed to the accepted idea of Marcus's bride, for the very idea of the wife of an Overton of Cranbrook Place holding down a job was unthinkable—at least, according to Marcus and his mother. And, although it was now hard to believe, at that particular time Petra had still been so blinded by her feelings for Marcus that she wanted only to make him happy, even though it had meant giving up her partnership with Di in Potpourri.

'May I ask why?' Adam's authoritative voice broke into her thoughts, snapping her back to the present, to the pleasant garden and this—this *inquisition*. 'Didn't you enjoy your work?'

She blinked at his bluntness. 'On the contrary,' she snapped, 'I loved it.'

'Ah.' He sat back, his arms folded. The sun glinted on his brown arms below the pushed-up sleeves of his sweater, and lit the fine, dark hairs above his wrist to copper wires. 'The business was failing, perhaps?'

'Certainly not!' she exclaimed. This man appeared to have no confidence in her at all! 'If you *must* know,' she flashed, 'we were doing well. Casterleigh was beginning to attract a lot of tourists. Americans fell in love with the abbey ruins and the castle. And a stately home nearby has recently opened its doors to the public so . . . Anyway, we didn't sell rubbish, but good, handcrafted stuff. I used to——' She broke off suddenly, biting her lip. There was no point in sounding defensive. Anyway, Adam Herrald wouldn't be interested in hearing about the miniature pressed-flower pictures and jewellery and greetings cards that she'd made in her flat above the shop. He'd damn the whole venture as something absurdly trivial and twee. She stifled an impulse to get up and walk away.

One eyebrow lifted fractionally. 'So,' he drawled, 'business was good. And you enjoyed it. Yet you sold out . . .?'

His faint question hung in the air for a moment. Really, she thought, he was impossible. Her past was none of his business. She lifted her short chin, glaring at him. 'I had my reasons. But I can't see that they have anything to do with *you.* Nor with this present job, which, as I understand it, entails caring for your sister's three children for the next few weeks. The fact that you and I have been thrown together doesn't give you the right to pry into my personal life.'

For a long moment they glared at each other, open enmity flaring between them in the calm afternoon. The amber light in Petra's eyes would have warned any of her friends not to press the matter further.

Then he shrugged. 'And that puts me firmly in my place,' he said scathingly.

Petra was quiet. I certainly hope so, she thought, But I doubt it. She poured more tea for herself, although she did not want it. But it gave her something to do, and—more important—something to look at, away from the burning bitterness in his eyes. She was pleased to see that her hands were steady and did not betray her outrage.

'And now I suppose there are a few questions you'd like to ask me,' he said, his voice moderating to a note of disinterest.

'Oh, I don't think so.' If he was conceited enough to think she was curious about him, he had sadly overestimated his importance. 'At the interview,' she went on smoothly, 'Mr Stansfield explained the situation—about your sister going into hospital. He also told me about the children's father being in the States on a lecture tour, and that you would be accompanying us to their grandmother's villa.' She gave him a challenging look. 'That's all I need to know, isn't it? However, I thought it could have been simplified if the children and I flew out to their grandmother's——'

'Sarah's afraid of flying,' he explained laconically. 'She's an imaginative child, and there was no point in making the situation worse for her. My assignment in Paris was almost complete, so I offered to drive them down, providing I had some back-up.'

'And from your remarks I gather you'd expected that back-up to be a nice, cosy, middle-aged, trained nanny.' Petra leaned back in the white chair and coolly brushed a crumb from her lap. 'Well, I'm sorry to disappoint you, Mr Herrald. And sorry, too, that you have no confidence in my abilities. But it seems you're stuck with me. Unless, of course,' she added spikily, 'you'd prefer to accept my resigna——'

'Damn it,' he growled, 'I'm in no position to indulge *my* preferences——'

'Although,' she went on, as if he hadn't spoken, 'I can't understand why you place such importance on age and appearance. I'm twenty-five, as you probably know. I've had some nursing experience—which included work with children—and I can assure you that I'm perfectly capable of seeing that the children have a good holiday without overtaxing their grandmother too much.' She paused for a moment, then went on softly, 'As I understood it, those were the requirements of the job. And as I seem to have satisfied both Mr Stansfield and Unity on that score, then I don't think *your* objections matter too much.'

He leaned an elbow on the table, resting his chin on his hand. 'Do go on, Miss Macey. I have the distinct feeling that you haven't finished yet.'

She ignored the heavy irony in his tone and went on smoothly, 'And I hope you won't think me impertinent, Mr Herrald, but in view of your very obvious disapproval of me, perhaps you should have made *your* conditions crystal clear, both to Unity and to Mr Stansfield. And then this situation would never have arisen, would it?' Ignoring his thunderous expression, she stood up, taking her handbag from the chair beside her.

He rose quickly, towering over her. 'Jack Stansfield and Unity know me well enough to—to take certain conditions as read,' he gritted.

For a moment they faced each other, the air between them as sensitive as an explosive charge. The power in his dark, furious figure was volcanic, threatening to erupt and overwhelm her. But she held on to the back of her chair as she stared into his eyes, and the strength of her resistance to him braced and upheld her. Blast this man and his attitudes! And what a stew he was making, when it was simply a case of her face not fitting. Well, that was *his* problem!

At last she tore her gaze away and drew a deep, steadying breath. 'And now,' she murmured with resolute politeness, 'if you'll excuse me, I'll go and see how my charges are getting on. By the way, do you wish me to arrange a light supper for Thomas so that he can go to bed early? And what are your instructions regarding Patrick and Sarah?'

'We're in France now, Miss Macey,' he snapped, 'where it seems usual for children to dine with the adults. When in Rome . . . You know the rest.'

'Very well. Although perhaps,' Petra pursued, with a mock-servility she couldn't resist, 'you'll prefer the hired help to take her meals separately.' A sudden, swift narrowing of his eyes fanned her spark of perversity, driving her on. 'I regret not having provided myself with the customary grey flannel uniform, but I thought the weather would be too warm.'

'Oh, for God's sake!' he grated. 'All I ask is that you do the job you've been engaged to do. What you wear doesn't interest me one bit.' The disdain in his eyes flicked her like a whip, but before she could speak he went on, 'And the children would think it odd if we didn't all eat together. After we get to the Villa des Roches their grandmother will make whatever arrangements she thinks fit. Once I've offloaded you and the children I'll be off on my own—most of the time, anyway.'

And thank heaven for that, Petra thought vehemently as she moved away, sensing his eyes watching her with open distaste.

She squared her slim shoulders. There was no alternative but to put up with him. After all, it would be for only three days, and once they arrived in the Ardèche she'd be pleased to see the back of him. In the meantime, she thought, seeking consolation, his company would at least be diluted by the presence of the children most of the time.

As she turned the corner of the building, following the direction the children had taken, she couldn't help comparing Adam Herrald's attitude with Mr Stansfield's pleasant manner at the interview in London. For within two minutes of walking into his office she'd felt instinctively that the job was hers. Mr Stansfield had taken to her immediately, engaging her on the spot despite four other applicants waiting in an outer office—some of whom, she conceded, appeared to resemble more closely Adam's idea of a suitable *type.* Her lip curled. Adam Herrald should have been born in an earlier age, she decided, when appearance was all.

She found Patrick and Thomas feeding lettuce to the rabbits in the company of a sturdy French boy, while Sarah sat on a step, crooning to a grey kitten curled in her lap. The door behind her stood open, and Petra could see into a vast, beamed kitchen where two women sat at a scrubbed table, slicing beans and chatting.

The scene had a relaxed timelessness which came as a relief to Petra after the turbulence of her scene with Adam, and she dropped thankfully down on the step beside Sarah. One of the maids got up and brought out a wooden kitchen chair, dusting it with her apron and gesturing smilingly.

'*Merci, madame.*' Petra smiled back and moved, although she would have preferred to be beside Sarah where she could lay a casual arm across Sarah's shoulders and know the girl's responsive affection towards a temporary substitute mother. For suddenly Petra, too, felt a sense of loneliness, almost of being bereft. She closed her eyes, feeling the sun warm on their lids. The sale of her share in Potpourri, then the unpleasant scenes with Marcus, and now, to top it all,

Adam Herrald's inexplicable hostility towards her, crowded in; she felt jittery and depressed.

She forced herself to unwind and respond to the summery scene around her, reminding herself that things would be different once they reached the Ardèche.

After a while she got up, calling to Thomas. 'As a holiday treat,' she told him, 'you'll be staying up late. So you ought to have a rest now. Let's go and see what a French bed feels like, hmm?' She held out her hand, then with a sudden surge of tenderness bent to pick him up. One warm hand crept round her neck and tugged her ear. Laughing, she turned the corner of the building, almost colliding with Adam. He made an instinctive movement of recoil, barely perceptible, but nevertheless there. She felt a hot blush storm into her face as he recovered almost immediately and reached out to ruffle Thomas's hair before moving on.

Completely baffled, she went slowly upstairs. What on earth was wrong with the man? Or—*wrong with her?* For surely such animosity as his had to stem from something deeper than mere disappointment that she wasn't the full-bosomed, matronly figure he'd anticipated. Her heart seemed to drop into an abyss; dining with him this evening would be another ordeal.

For a moment she considered the possibility of pleading a headache and asking for an omelette to be sent up to her in her room. But then she dismissed the idea as cowardly subterfuge. It wouldn't be fair to the children. Nor would it do her image any good in Adam Herrald's eyes. Not that she cared about that; but, she realised with a stab of irritation, those unfathomable eyes would see right through her ruse. And she sensed he wouldn't let her get away with it.

Resolutely she turned her mind away from all thoughts of him as she pottered quietly around the room while Thomas slept. Later, as the children dressed, she was at pains to see that there was nothing about their appearance which could give rise to criticism.

She showered quickly in the tiny bathroom, and changed into an ivory skirt and matching silk shirt, its plainness relieved only by rows of tiny pintucks. Then she went down, trying to flatten the flutter of trepidation inside her.

Turning the curve of the wide staircase she saw Adam below, standing at a small bar at one end of the long dining-room. Thomas called out, and Adam turned. His eyes held Petra's for a long moment. She felt stunned, almost as if he'd reached out, gripping her with a potent force that paralysed her in a world that had suddenly stopped. Then she read in his gaze a mute signal of armed neutrality.

Giving herself a slight shake, she went on down on feet that felt leaden. She saw that he, too, had changed, into a grey silk sweater and matching trousers topped by a white jacket. Even among the sprinkling of well-dressed guests he stood out, seeming to diminish the others. And with a reluctant sense of capitulation Petra realised that even if she hadn't known him her eyes would have been drawn instinctively to the tall, perfectly proportioned figure. Its suggestion of a latent, casual grace overlying a magnetic core at once attracted her, yet—at the same time—repelled because of its very strength. No man had the right to so much . . . charisma, she thought despondently. Especially when it was purely superficial.

'An aperitif, Miss Macey?' he murmured as she

reached him.

She gave a tight smile. 'No, thank you. I'm on duty, remember?'

To her surprise, he laughed. She saw that one of his teeth was very slightly uneven along its edge, lending to his smile the attractive, humorous curl she'd noticed earlier. Not that he had favoured *her* with it, she reflected wryly. 'Oh, I hope you're not going to be stuffy,' he remarked in velvet tones. 'When in Rome . . .'

'You've said that once already,' she told him stiffly.

'But it bears repeating, I think. Or don't you *ever* have to be told anything twice?' His smile was still there, maddeningly superior, but his words were barbed.

'Not where you're concerned, Mr Herrald,' she answered. 'I'm quite clear about *your* requirements.' If he thought he could grill her as unpleasantly as he had during the afternoon, then suddenly disarm her with a spurious charm, he was quite wrong. She'd got the message loud and clear. If a nanny figure was what he wanted, she'd do her best to oblige. And let him save his charm for women who weren't forewarned by the knowledge of his darker side.

But if he noticed the prickle in her voice he gave no indication of it. 'They keep an excellent cellar here,' he remarked conversationally, 'and I've ordered the wine for our meal.' He turned towards the bar, and she was left staring at the broad, white-clad shoulders, the stamp of authority written in the very set of his head. A moment later he was handing down two glasses to the children, who exclaimed with delight at the bright rosy colour. 'Grenadine,' he explained. 'You'll like it. Why not take it outside on the terrace? Patrick's already there.'

'I'd rather stay with Petra,' Sarah said, and Thomas echoed her.

Silently Petra blessed them both. Adam Herrald angry was bad enough. But that was a threat she could deal with. Now, in the relaxed atmosphere of pre-dinner drinks, the threat was still there. But it emanated from a softer, more disturbing source. And despite herself his magnetism touched her, drew her . . .

Then he was holding out a glass. 'Your aperitif,' he said firmly. 'So drink it. It might help you to relax.' His eyes held a taunting glint.

'I'm perfectly relaxed,' Petra protested. 'Is there any reason why I shouldn't be?' She stared up at him; how did one hide from dark eyes which saw too much?

'Oh? Then why do you keep fiddling with your finger in that irritating way?'

Too late she realised that she was lightly massaging the place where, for three months, Marcus's ring had been. As her lips opened to frame a retort he said very quietly, so that only she heard, 'Look, Miss Macey, shall we try to make this part of the holiday as pleasant as possible? For the children's sake?'

It was a question, but it rang like an order and, defeated, she could only nod. He was right, of course—at least in that respect.

Almost against her will she found that she was relaxing as the day's tensions receded.

Dinner was delicious, and she discovered that Adam shared her passion for seafood. Conversation was general and included the children to the extent where, after a while, they were doing most of the talking.

The long room with its small windows grew shadowy as twilight thickened outside. The napery and glasses gleamed in the golden light of table-lamps, and a sense of tranquillity slid over Petra, smoothing out the frictions that had bedevilled her since meeting Adam. At least for the duration of the meal it seemed to Petra that her problems were less pressing, as Adam effortlessly led the talk into channels which kept the children amused. It was a skilful strategy, she realised approvingly, engaging their interest and keeping their minds off thoughts of home and their mother who, at this very moment, was probably in the operating theatre.

The service was pleasantly unhurried, and Petra thought suddenly what a perfect setting this would make for a lovers' meeting. It seemed that the old grey stones exuded the perfume of past romances into the softly lit room; only the violins were missing. Her lips twitched, then she caught Adam's gaze upon her, warily speculative. She lifted her glass to her lips, giving back a blank stare over its rim.

Despite her earlier resolution, her thoughts were dragged back to the last time she'd dined with Marcus. The service then had been slow, too. 'But there's no hurry,' she'd protested as he began to fume silently, his mouth drawn into a downturn. He'd been brusque to the waiter, and had finally sent for the manager. It had all been most embarrassing. She couldn't imagine Marcus in this setting; he'd see the Lion d'Or as an inconvenient old place with antiquated plumbing. He'd consider the shellfish suspect, and by now he'd be drumming his fingers on the table, his head sinking into his shoulders as he grew more and more dissatisfied.

The wonder was, how could she ever have been so blind as to contemplate marriage to him? To him and his mother, she added silently. For that was how it would have been.

She was rubbing her finger again, almost as if she wanted to erase the memory of that ring—a square-cut emerald because all Overton brides had worn square-cut emeralds.

Annoyed at herself for indulging in pointless memories, she clasped her hands loosely on the table and glanced up to meet Adam's slightly amused gaze. She wished she'd chosen any other place to sit but opposite him. Somehow it made her vulnerable, too conscious of the spotlight of his scrutiny. His gaze moved down to her left hand and the faint white mark against her tan, then back to her face again thoughtfully.

She felt a warm blush rise as she hurriedly moved her hands to her lap. The children were counting cherry stones on their plates, arguing and laughing.

'Just for a moment, Miss Macey, you looked almost—hunted.' Adam's voice was low, almost inaudible, yet each syllable reached her clearly.

'Are you suggesting now that I might be some sort of criminal?' she whispered. 'A fugitive?'

The mobile eyebrows rose fractionally. 'Not at all,' he drawled. 'It was merely an idle observation. What a sensitive lady you are. I can see I'll have to be very careful what I say to you. My apologies if I've touched a painful spot.' She felt that he was laughing at her, and she looked away quickly.

'You haven't,' she returned crisply, putting down her napkin and turning to the children. 'If you've finished, I think it's time for bed. *All* of you,' she went on firmly as she saw that Patrick was about to argue. She felt that she was being unfair in using them because of her own sudden need to escape from an atmosphere that was rapidly becoming oppressive.

But, after all, it *was* late, and they'd had a long and eventful day.

'Miss Macey's right,' Adam said, glancing at his watch. 'Off you go. Sarah, you can see to Thomas. It won't be the first time, I know. Miss Macey and I will take coffee together, then we'll be up. By then you should all be asleep.'

'Oh, but——' Petra's eyes dropped away from his compelling stare. The very last thing she wanted was to be alone with him. Until these last few minutes the evening had been agreeably free of hostile undercurrents. And she'd no wish to ruin it all now, establishing an unpleasant basis for the following day.

'Why do you call her *Miss Macey?*' Thomas said plaintively. 'We call her *Petra.*'

'Because,' Petra interposed quickly, 'I *work* for your mummy. I'm not a—a friend, you see. More of a—well, a help . . .'

'You're *my* friend,' Thomas said stoutly. 'Anyway, Mrs Maggs works for Mummy. *She* helps, and Mummy calls her *Lily*——'

'And Dad calls her "that imbecile",' Patrick put in with a grin. ' "Where's that imbecile put my tobacco jar?" he says.'

Petra laughed, grateful for the nugget of gossip which had turned the talk away from herself. 'Say goodnight to your uncle, then,' she prompted. 'I'll come up with you.'

'No coffee?' Adam said. Petra thought she heard a note of relief in his voice. Perhaps the offer had been made out of politeness and he, too, was glad to drop the pretence.

'It would keep me awake,' she said lightly.

'We'll have an early start tomorrow,' he said. 'So, breakfast at eight-fifteen. And be ready to leave immediately afterwards,' he added flatly.

'Of course, Mr Herrald. You can count on me.' She flashed him a sweet, demure smile.

He turned away quickly, his face unreadable. 'I hope so, Miss Macey. I certainly hope so.'

Did she imagine it, or was there a note of warning in his voice? 'Goodnight,' she said tartly, and followed the children out.

CHAPTER TWO

IT SEEMED that Petra had slept for only a few hours before Sarah was rousing her urgently. She sat up in bed with a start, glanced at her watch and groaned, throwing back the covers. Almost eight! And not for anything was she going to give Adam cause for complaint.

She chivvied the two children, who dawdled infuriatingly while she completed the packing, and when she hurried them downstairs it was twelve minutes past eight. Made it, she thought triumphantly, hastily knotting the drawstring belt of her dress.

In the hall Thomas stopped suddenly, remembering that he'd left his blue elephant on his bed. 'We'll have to get it,' Sarah complained. 'He never goes anywhere without it.'

'You two go on out to the terrace,' Petra said. 'I'll nip up and fetch it.'

Turning to go back, she saw that in the alcove beneath the stairs Adam stood with his back towards her. He was speaking quietly into the telephone, but the clarity of his diction in the silent hall brought every word softly to her. 'Great news,' he said. 'Wonderful. Yes . . . Fine. I'll tell the children and call the hospital myself later. And maybe . . .'

Petra's feet made no noise on the stairs as she passed on out of hearing. It sounded as if he were speaking of Unity, and from that fragment of conversation it looked as if the operation was over and all was well.

I'll ring Di tonight, Petra decided, and ask her to organise some flowers for Unity. In the brief time she'd spent with the children's mother she'd warmed to her, for Unity had the knack of putting people instantly at their ease. And Petra had admired her sense of humour and her philosophy of taking things as they came and not worrying too much. It had even helped Petra to put her own problems into perspective, temporarily at least.

How different Unity was from Adam, she reflected ruefully, picking up the blue velvet elephant and closing the bedroom door quietly behind her.

As she neared the curve of the stairs she could hear that he was still talking. But now his tone was sharper and perfunctory. '... don't know what the hell you were thinking of, Jack. What? Oh, come on, man, you must have guessed how I'd ... Yes. All *right*. I know all that, but when I need a shrink I'll find a professional. I've had enough of amateur psychotherapy over the past couple of years to last me a lifetime, well meant though it no doubt was. And at a guess I'd say Unity was in on it. Well? Was she?'

He was silent for a moment, apparently listening. Petra hesitated, uncertain about hurrying out to the children in case Adam turned round and saw her. He'd know then that she must have overheard what was clearly a very private conversation. She made a little moue. That would make a bad start to the day. She felt nervous enough as it was. She could visualise his face hardening, the taut olive skin gleaming over the granite cheekbones. He'd look at her with those bleak, black eyes, and she'd already experienced their withering, inhibiting effect. On the other hand, if she went back to her room and waited about she'd be late for breakfast. Either way she was sunk.

She'd just decided to make a quick dash to the terrace when she froze, gripped by his next words. 'Well, of *course* she's all right with the kids. They like her. But . . . Well, how many applicants were there? I see. And do you mean to tell me that out of that lot you couldn't find anyone else just as capable? It must have been obvious to you that I'd . . . What? Damn it, I'd have thought that you, Jack, of all people, would——'

Petra waited no longer. Blindly she turned and stumbled back up to the bedroom, closing the door behind her and sinking shakily on to the bed. He'd been talking—to Mr Stansfield—about *her*! That much was crystal-clear, even if the rest of the conversation wasn't. Something else was painfully obvious, too; until now she hadn't fully understood the sheer intensity of his dislike.

She shook her head, dazed. But *why* did he feel so strongly against her? *Why?* What had she *done*, for heaven's sake?

She crouched on the bed, absently crushing the little elephant between her hands, trying to grapple with the thoughts that tumbled through her brain. Certainly she'd stood up to him yesterday afternoon, so that might be the reason . . . But, she remembered, his animosity had been apparent earlier, from the first moment of meeting, in fact. He'd taken an instant dislike to her, for no better reason than that she didn't look like the conventional nanny. At least, that was his explanation.

She stared at her strained reflection in the mirror. The truth of the matter was that she didn't actually have to do anything; she didn't have to give him a reason to feel the way he did. She just had to be herself, and that was enough. *'I do not like thee, Doctor*

Fell; The reason why I cannot tell . . .' The jingle ticked sickeningly through her mind, repeating itself over and over. It was completely baffling. And so unfair. That a mature man should make such a hasty, irrational judgement was beyond comprehension! Or could it be that in spite of his flair and panache he *wasn't* mature? Was that it? He'd spoken of psychotherapy . . . So was there some flaw in his psychological make-up? After all, what did she really know about him?

She tore her gaze away from her reflection and stared unseeingly at a tendril of creeper tapping the window outside. She'd known little more than his name when she left the interview; his name and the fact that he would be driving her and the children. And it was only when she'd got back to Casterleigh, and on her way up to her flat had stopped in at the shop to tell Di she'd got the job, that she'd learned just whom she'd be travelling with.

Petra saw it all again: Di carefully putting down the etched goblet she was pricing and saying with slow incredulity, 'You mean *the* Adam Herrald? What a break! A man like that!'

'Like what?' Petra had stared. 'Do you know him? *Is* he something special?'

'I should say so! And I know *of* him. He's a photographer. I've seen his work in the glossiest of the glossy magazines.' Di had closed her eyes ecstatically. 'Impossibly willowy women modelling fabulous, unaffordable clothes . . . Artistic or bizarre studies of jet-setters . . . And the backgrounds! French châteaux, Italian palazzi, the Bahamas, coral reefs, Greek tavernas . . . Oh, you *must* have seen his work!'

Petra had laughed. 'Maybe I have. But apparently it made more impression on you than it did on me.'

'One of the Sunday colour supplements ran an article on him a few months ago . . .' Di had frowned. 'I wish I could remember more about him. But there was a photo of him looking all black and strong—rather like a latter-day Heathcliff . . .' Her eyes narrowed. 'So,' she purred, 'I'd say you're in for a ve-ry interesting time, Pet.'

Recalling that conversation now, Petra winced and got up. She could do without the kind of interest that Adam Herrald was providing.

For several minutes her hurt battled with her anger. All her instincts warned her to leave, to invent some excuse and make her way back to Dieppe, then England . . .

But running out on the children was no way of fulfilling the trust that Unity and Mr Stansfield had placed in her—although judging from Adam's telephone conversation even that now seemed to be suspect, and certainly not quite so straightforward as it had seemed at the interview.

No, deserting the children wasn't the answer. She couldn't even consider it. She'd stay, she decided, setting her mouth stubbornly, stay and do the job she'd undertaken. Hurt melted away, scorched by a sudden flare of anger. To hell with Adam Herrald and his hang-ups! If he was so very selective then he should have moved heaven and earth to be at the interview instead of whingeing because Jack Stansfield had engaged the wrong person.

She looked at her watch. She'd been hiding up here for almost ten minutes. Surely Adam would have finished his phone call by now. But if he hadn't, what did it matter?

Despite the stiffening effect of her bravado she was a little dismayed to see that he was already with the children at a table on the terrace. It was relatively simple to be hard-headed and objective about him when he wasn't there, she thought sinkingly, but the sight of those shoulders, the proud, dark head and close-set ears, and the negligent figure loosely graceful in any posture, was daunting. Already she felt her carefully repaired composure eroding.

He rose. 'Good morning, Miss Macey,' he said in glacial tones. 'You'll forgive us for having started without you.' Two dark spots of colour burned on his cheekbones, and his lips hardly moved as he clipped out the words. Petra wondered if he was still angry with Jack Stansfield. Or was it simply because she was late? Disobeyed his orders? Well, if he was looking for an apology, he could forget it.

'Oh, that's all right,' she said, forcing a sunny smile, sliding into a chair and dropping Thomas's elephant on to his lap.

'You've been *ages*,' Thomas bubbled. 'And Adam's going to see if we can talk to Mummy on the telephone tonight.'

'Yes.' Sarah tossed back her ponytail, her eyes huge and shining. 'She's had her operation. Adam's been talking to Uncle Jack.'

'Really?' Petra's eyebrows arched interestedly as she turned to Adam. 'That is good news. I hope everything is going well. And children, I've had an idea. How about each of you keeping a journal of this holiday? Then when you see your mother she'll be able to read about what you did and the things you saw on the journey.'

'But Thomas can't write,' Patrick pointed out sensibly.

'He can draw, though. And I'll help. And Patrick, if you've finished, go up and clean your teeth, please.'

She gave a bright, wide smile. It felt like a grimace. 'You, too, Sarah. You know that your uncle is planning an early start.'

With neat, sure movements she poured coffee for herself and broke a croissant with brisk, efficient fingers. 'I promise you won't be kept waiting on my account.' The polite smile she gave Adam hurt. She wanted to shout and scream at him, demanding an explanation so that she could defend herself against his unfair prejudice.

He flashed her a narrowed look, frowned and glanced away as if the sight of her offended him. Then, putting down his cup, he said, 'I'll go and settle the bill, then.' He got up, and instantly she was aware of his lithe, lazy grace. 'Shall we say—twenty minutes?'

'Fine.' She gave all her attention to spreading quince jelly on her croissant.

Already the morning was warm, promising a fine day. The sun shone on the recently watered tubs of flowers, trapping tiny diamonds among them. But Petra felt cold and exhausted. The day stretched endlessly ahead. 'Come along, Thomas,' she coaxed numbly. 'Finish your breakfast quickly. We mustn't keep them waiting.'

Fortunately there was no need for more than the most desultory remarks during the early part of the day's drive. Petra tried to occupy her mind by helping Thomas with a construction kit while simultaneously playing a paper game with Patrick. Sarah, in the front passenger seat, pored over maps and issued wrong instructions in an important voice which Adam corrected with good humour. There seemed every reason why the children *should* be fond of him, Petra conceded. After all, even a rotten apple usually had one or two good spots.

From beneath lowered lashes she stole a glance at him. His shirt-cuffs were turned loosely back, revealing strong wrists and brown, shapely hands. Elegance, she reflected idly, was an adjective usually associated with women. But he had an elegance that was almost aggressively masculine, from his hand-made loafers up to the dark hair winging thickly back from the taut, almost Slavonic, temples.

Inwardly she laughed; he wouldn't take kindly to being compared with a rotten apple. Then she remembered his telephone conversation. There was nothing to laugh at at all. The chill in her stomach renewed itself like a cold kind of indigestion.

However, when they stopped for coffee at a pavement café she was unable to avoid direct conversation with him any longer. 'We should make Beaugency by one,' he said, glancing at his watch. 'I know of a decent restaurant there for lunch.'

'Actually, I'd thought of a picnic,' Petra said, with a note of authority in her voice. Then, as Thomas whispered, 'Ooh, yes,' she went on, 'Our main meal is in the evening, so a light lunch would be better for the children. However——' and again she summoned up that wide, false smile '—naturally, that doesn't have to involve you. I'd hate to upset your plans. So if you'd drop us off at a suitable spot we'll picnic on the riverbank, and you can go off to your restaurant.'

'Oh? You know that Beaugency's on the Loire, then?'

Don't patronise me, Mr High-and-Mighty, she thought acidly. And only the children's presence prevented her from saying it. 'Of course,' she snapped. 'I, too, can read a map.'

'I'm sure you can do a lot of things, Miss Macey.

But naturally, I'll be eating with you,' he said silkily.

She lifted a slim, graceful shoulder. 'As you wish,' she said carelessly. 'Sarah and I will do the shopping, then. Any particular instructions?'

He regarded her coldly for a moment, then said, 'Oh, I have every confidence in your ability to organise a simple picnic lunch.'

'There's a toyshop along the street,' Patrick blurted out. 'May we go and look?'

'Yes, run along if you've finished your drinks,' Adam said before Petra could protest.

After the children had gone, the silence pricked between them. Petra concentrated her gaze on a girl in pink Bermuda shorts picking over melons outside a fruit shop opposite. But she was deeply conscious of Adam's dark eyes watching her broodingly, and as if in response to his stare a blush rose in a warm tide, suffusing her face. And she knew that he'd noticed. Then he said, in quiet tones but with an underlying flash of steel, 'All right. Let's have it, Miss Macey. What's the trouble now?'

She flung round quickly. The nerve of him, the duplicity! She thrust down a desire to spring to her feet, lean across the table and shout out just what 'the trouble' was. For one reckless moment she tasted the pleasure of telling him that she'd overheard his conversation with Jack Stansfield. Just to see his face would be some recompense, for surely even he wouldn't be able to conceal his shame.

But she'd have to deny herself that pleasure; he would immediately damn her as an eavesdropper—in addition to all her other shortcomings, whatever they were. She took a steadying sip of coffee, controlled the urge, then said coolly, '*Is* there any trouble?' She raised her eyes, watching him with a glint of ice in their hazel depths.

'You tell me.' His tone was dry. 'I thought we had an agreement.' As she raised her eyebrows, he went on, 'You seem to have forgotten that we made a deal to bury the hatchet for the duration of this journey, purely for the children's sake.'

'Hatchet?' she said politely. 'Oh, so you do admit that there *is* one.'

A quick frown of impatience narrowed his eyes, and he shifted in his chair, the movement tightening his thigh muscles for an instant. Quickly Petra looked away. 'Oh, do stop prevaricating,' he ground out. 'From your behaviour, it seems that there is.'

She gave a tinkle of laughter. How devious he was! Yesterday—apart from during dinner—he'd treated her as if she were some kind of pariah. Yet now he had the nerve to accuse *her* of being difficult.

'I don't think I follow you,' she murmured. 'What exactly have I done wrong now? Let me remind you that my commitment is to the children, and they seem perfectly happy.' Ice-chips sparkled in her narrowed eyes. 'And if *they've* no cause for complaint, I can't see that *you* have.'

She moved her arm to put down her cup. But suddenly her hand was stopped in mid-air as he gripped her wrist, his fingers locking strongly around the delicate bone. She gasped, unprepared for the sudden leaping response of her blood. A sense of shock tingled through her, and she stared at him, her eyes widening.

He gave her arm a little shake. 'You know damn well what I mean,' he hissed. 'All this—this—*froth.* You're sulking over something, and you're trying to hide it. Your brittle, assumed brightness, this pose of——'

She flung off his hand. 'Do you mind?' she blazed. 'Kindly stop—manhandling me. I am *not* your chattel. So what gives you the right to think you can dictate my moods? No, don't answer that; your reply would only bore me. But just remember this, Mr——'

To her mounting fury he began to laugh, the low, smoky sound of amusement she'd heard before. 'So,' he said with creamy satisfaction, 'I've got through to you at last!' He leaned back in his chair, leisurely enjoying the sight of her anger. Her eyes sparked like goldstones, the blush still stained her cheeks under the pale tan. And her heart seemed to have found a crazy rhythm of its own. 'Do you know, Miss Macey,' he went on in a confidential purr, 'I do believe I prefer the little hellcat to that neat, shiny automaton of the breakfast-table.'

'So?' she flashed. 'What makes you think I give a damn how you prefer me? I've never been less interested . . . Your opinion—which might seem sacred to you—means nothing. Why should it? I don't have enough respect for you to care one way or the other.' Her fists were tightly clenched on her lap. His laughter was the last straw. It would have given her the greatest pleasure to slap that autocratic face, now softened in lines of amusement. 'So far as I'm concerned, you're merely the driver. And now, if you don't mind, I'll join the children. I prefer their company. Then Sarah and I will do the shopping. And I do hope that lunch will be to your liking, although I don't expect I'll lose any sleep if it isn't.'

Infuriatingly, he ignored her outburst. He was still watching her, one eyebrow slightly raised. His mouth still held its attractive, crooked smile. 'Just as you say,' he murmured. 'And you might send Thomas and

Patrick back here to me. We'll go and fill up with petrol. Meet us outside the church, right? Oh, and you'll need this,' he went on, standing up and taking out his wallet to hand her a note. 'For the food.' He pressed it into her palm and closed her fingers over it, his touch scalding her.

Then his voice hardened. 'And do, please, bear that agreement in mind, Miss Macey.' The smile was gone; baffling eyes watched her from under long, slumbrous lids, the thick lashes almost touching and tangling. 'I'm sure that with your vast experience of caring for children,' he said with heavy sarcasm, 'you don't need me to tell you that they can be very sensitive to atmosphere, particularly Sarah. And let's get this straight,' he went on, looming over her so that his size and strength seemed to threaten her, forcing her to step backwards, 'nothing, but *nothing* is going to spoil this journey for them. Is that understood?' He reached out suddenly and put a hard forefinger under her chin, jerking up her head roughly, his eyes imprisoning her gaze. 'So just remember it, will you? And in case you still haven't got my drift, that's an order.'

Impatiently Petra wrenched her head away. 'Is it really?' she said, her words dropping like sharp pebbles. 'Then all I can say is that it's a tall one. And one that your manner makes it very difficult to obey.'

His hand fell to his side, but his eyes still held hers in an ebony trap. They seemed to be the only two people in the sunny street, locked to each other by their eyes, shackled by mutual loathing. 'Is that so?' he drawled. 'Then you'll just have to try very, very hard. Won't you, Miss Macey?'

She turned sharply, breaking the invisible chains

and flinging herself away from him. The man was insufferable! She blinked back tears of frustration, slowing her steps as she neared the children still clustered outside the toyshop. She simply must compose herself before she reached them. She bit her lip to control its shaking. However reluctant she was to admit it, he was right: children *were* sensitive to atmosphere, and didn't she, too, want them to enjoy this hateful journey? But it was going to take a superhuman effort on her part to put aside her dislike of their uncle. Yet she had no choice but to grit her teeth and comply. And he knew it.

She did manage a pale smile as she joined the children, then she tucked Sarah's arm in hers and sent the two boys back to the café, where Adam was dropping a few coins on to a saucer. 'Bread,' she said to Sarah. 'Two *baguettes* should do us. Some ham and cheese and tomatoes. Peaches, I think, and five——'

'Strawberry tarts?' Sarah suggested hopefully.

'Exactly what I was going to say.' She was rewarded by Sarah's delighted laugh, and she felt the tight knot inside her ease a little.

It was shortly after one when they crossed the Loire and found a picnic spot on the bank of the river. Adam parked close by and unearthed a couple of rugs from the depths of one of the lockers in the camper, and the children carried the food and crockery down towards the water's edge. Thomas had brought a small plastic boat, and he pottered on the shingly bank while Patrick raised his telescope to survey a preening swan on one of the little islands.

'I'll be back in a few minutes,' Adam said suddenly, after he'd spread the rugs. Petra nodded a reply, stifling a desire to tell him not to hurry. As she and Sarah split and buttered the long bread sticks she still couldn't trust herself to speak amiably to him, although since the coffee-break his manner had been easy and informal towards her.

She turned away from slicing tomatoes to glance at Thomas. Then, even as she watched, she saw the red boat bob out of reach, his arm stretched out, his fingers starfish-spread . . . Then the splash of his small body falling forward.

Fear thickened in her throat as she flung down the knife and hurled herself after him, grabbing the back of his T-shirt and sprawling beside him in the water.

Then she gave an unsteady laugh that was a half-sob. With the horror-waves still rippling through her, she felt her knees touch the gravelly bottom. The water was about a foot deep! Half laughing, half crying, she pulled him upright, her other hand reaching out for the little boat. 'You gave me such a fright,' she whispered, holding him firmly. 'Don't ever do that again, Thomas.' Her breath came raggedly as she hugged him. Oh, God, it could have been so different . . . Deeper water, a strong undertow . . . It didn't bear thinking about.

Thomas was shrieking with laughter as he squeezed the water out of his shorts, encouraged by the mirth of the other two on the bank. 'I drowned,' he crowed. 'Didn't I drown, Petra?'

'Not quite, but you're very wet. Patrick, throw me the car keys, please. I'll take Thomas back to the camper and change. And neither of you two move an inch. Promise? Come along, Thomas, let's get out of these wet things.'

Inside the camper she dried him briskly and found him clean shorts, shirt and fresh sneakers. Then she combed his hair and sent him up to the front while she changed. Quickly she stripped, drying herself and crouching so that she couldn't be seen by any passing motorists. Hurriedly she dragged on panties and bra, and was reaching for the skirt she'd put out when the side door opened.

For an endless moment she stared up into Adam's amused face. Then she leaned forward to snatch up the towel and clutch it in front of her.

'Well, well,' he murmured, half closed eyes flickering over her slowly, 'I've heard of *The Naked Lunch*, but I didn't think that I'd——'

'Oh, shut *up*,' she breathed. She was beyond making the effort of self-control. He *would* have to turn up just now! And not only had he caught her looking distraught and haunted by that near-tragedy, but embarrassingly half dressed. 'Anyway,' she sparked, 'I'm not naked.'

'No, not quite,' he agreed softly, his eyes lingering on her bare shoulders. She realised then that in her half-crouching position the lacy bra that only partially skimmed her breasts gave him a bird's eye view of her soft curves. She raised the towel, still glaring at him.

'A gentleman,' she said scathingly, 'would have turned away.' Adam actually seemed to enjoy prolonging her humiliation.

'And a lady,' he taunted, 'would have closed the curtains.'

Before she could think of a suitable retort, Thomas turned to kneel on the front seat, peering over the back. 'I drowned, Adam,' he shouted.

'Did you, indeed?' Adam glanced sharply at Thomas, then back to Petra's face. She read the accusation in his stare and waited, watching him and dreading the return of his cold condemnation of her.

Then he reached past her. 'I presume this comes next,' he said, passing her the black T-shirt.

'Thank you,' she mumbled, half turning from him and dragging it over her head.

'And now . . . this?'

She nodded, not trusting herself to speak as she stepped into the flowered skirt and zipped it up.

'Well?' he said caustically. 'I suppose you do intend to tell me just what happened?'

Petra swallowed and said in a small voice, 'Thomas was sailing his boat. I was watching . . . But it was all so sudden. He—fell. Into the water . . . And I threw myself after him and——'

'Very noble of you,' Adam said drily, 'if a trifle over-zealous, considering how shallow the river is just there.'

'I didn't know that, did I?' she flared. 'I didn't stop to think. I acted instinctively, just . . . did the first thing that . . .' She turned away quickly from his expressionless scrutiny. Tears shone in her eyes, for now that everything was all right she felt weak and spent. Relief mingled with the terrifying might-have-been images of shelving banks, clutching weeds, swift, deadly currents . . . And Thomas, so small . . . And in her charge.

If Adam Herrald had wanted justification of his lack of confidence in her, he certainly had it now, she thought dismally. She dashed a hand across her eyes and fumbled blindly for her comb.

'Thomas.' Adam turned to the boy who was staring at Petra in shocked fascination. 'In that cupboard you'll find plastic tumblers. Take five of them, will you, down to the others? And don't go near the water until we come. All right?'

Then he went forward and reached into the glove

compartment and found a silver hipflask. 'Brandy,' he said, as Petra dropped her head into her hands. 'Take a little. You look as if you need it. Come on.' A little spike of humour touched his voice. 'And please don't tell me that you don't drink on duty.'

Petra glanced up at him. She didn't trust his concern for her. In a moment she'd feel the whiplash of his tongue. But he was watching her with a faint smile as he held out the flask.

She drew a deep, shuddering breath. 'Th—thank you. I'm sorry. You must think that I'm . . .' Her words died as she remembered exactly what he *did* think of her. Her voice hardened again. 'I *was* watching Thomas, but it all happened too quickly to——'

'Yes,' said Thomas, clutching the tumblers importantly, 'quick as a trick.'

'Off you go,' Adam said, and Thomas jumped out of the camper. Petra still sat, staring down at the hipflask, and Adam dropped into the seat beside her. She was conscious of his closeness. She even seemed to feel the warmth of his body like a reassurance. But that was a delusion. Now that Thomas was safely out of hearing Adam would let her have it, good and strong. She took a long drink of the brandy and choked a little. Then, wiping her eyes, she handed the flask back.

'All right, now?' As she nodded, Adam went on, 'Put it behind you. If that's the worst thing that happens to young Thomas he'll lead a charmed life.' Then he went on crisply, 'So get a grip on yourself. I'm hungry. Your hair's all right, so stop fiddling with it.' He turned away abruptly and stood up. 'And perhaps now,' he said tonelessly, 'you'll realise that you're not quite so capable as you'd have me believe, for—'

'I've said I'm sorry,' she began. 'I know it's—'

'Because,' he went on inexorably, 'you forgot to buy the drinks. Didn't you, Miss Macey? Wine for us, orange for the children.'

For a moment she stared at him, her lips parted. Then she saw that he'd put a plastic carrier bag on the floor, from which protruded the neck of a bottle. A glimmer of a smile danced in the dark depths of his eyes, and she answered it with a tentative grin.

'That's better,' he said. 'Now all we need is a corkscrew.'

As they walked down towards the river she still felt a little unsteady, but she was calmer and, strangely, comforted. Adam had found the right note, even contriving to lighten the situation with a little humour. And somehow he'd managed to put the whole thing into the perspective of a mere incident in a small boy's life.

But that wouldn't be the end of it. Once the day was over and the children out of the way, the whole thing would be brutally resurrected, and she wouldn't be let off lightly. She owed her reprieve to nothing more than his intention to maintain an atmosphere of harmony for the children's sakes.

Subdued, she avoided looking at him during lunch, concentrating instead on the children. After they'd eaten Adam lay back, his hands locked behind his head. 'Ten minutes,' he said lazily, 'then we must be on our way.'

Sarah carefully buried her peach stone, then said thoughtfully, 'I'm so lucky.'

'Oh?' Adam murmured. 'How do you make that out?'

'Well, I'm missing school, aren't I?' She rolled over

on to her stomach.

'You'll have to make up for it when you get back,' Petra warned her with a smile. 'You mightn't feel so lucky then.'

Sarah grinned back. 'I know. But just at this very moment there's only one thing I'm sorry about—apart from Mummy, I mean.'

'And what's that?' Petra asked, stacking the tumblers.

'I'll miss Tracey Lovat's sister's wedding. Tracey's my special friend, and she's going to be a bridesmaid. She's got a dress of peach silk and a little crown of flowers. I was going to see her.'

'Great stuff!' Patrick scoffed. 'Weddings!'

Sarah withered him with a glance of her brown eyes. Then she looked across at Adam. 'I'd like to be a bridesmaid,' she said. 'I'd have a dress of greeny-blue. Adam? She frowned thoughtfully. 'If you get married—again, I mean—may I be a bridesmaid?'

Petra's hands froze around the plates she was collecting. She dared not look at Adam. Oh, be careful, Sarah, she implored silently. I'm sure you've said the wrong thing.

Her hands began to move again, as if of their own volition. Married? Adam Herrald? That had never occured to her. It had come as a shock. But why, she wondered? Why should it? There was no logical reason why she should have ever given the matter a thought. And, anyway, no reason why it should be of interest now.

It was just that . . . that she'd assumed he was a bachelor.

She thought at first that Adam hadn't heard Sarah's question, but after an uncomfortable pause he said blandly, 'Of course. But don't set your hopes too high. I've no immediate plans in that direction.'

After a moment he stood up. 'Everyone ready, then?' He brushed a few shreds of grass from his trousers, his face hidden from Petra, picked up the rugs and went ahead of them back to the camper.

Petra stared after him. So it hadn't been imagination; Sarah had obviously touched on a very delicate subject, one that Adam certainly hadn't welcomed.

'Do you think he's cross with me?' Sarah asked, perplexed.

Petra gave the ponytail a reassuring tug. 'Oh, I shouldn't think so. But it might be best not to mention it again.'

'I only saw her once,' Sarah confided. 'Her name was Merrill. She had long auburn hair. I didn't like her much.'

'Will you carry the plates?' Petra felt it was important to steer right away from the subject. Adam was already in the driving seat, his profile obscured by an unfolded map, and when they joined him he was silent.

But as they drove south into the Allier countryside Petra found her mind unable to resist speculation. What had happened? Divorce? That wasn't so unusual these days. And after all, she thought with a touch of asperity, any woman with an ounce of spirit would have her work cut out coping with that lordly manner, that aloofness behind which Adam seemed able to immure himself against anyone whom he chose to dislike.

And that, of course, included *her*.

Dully she reminded herself that she still hadn't paid the price of allowing Thomas to fall into the river. And Sarah's indiscretion hadn't done anything to improve his mood. No doubt she'd get the full force of it later. He was simply biding his time.

CHAPTER THREE

BY HALF-PAST six they were settled in at a hotel just outside Moulins, and by seven o'clock the children were jostling for turns to speak to their mother on the telephone as Petra dressed for dinner.

She took great care with her appearance for no other reason, she told herelf, than that of needing to bolster her self-confidence. She was wishing heartily that, instead of making this journey by the more picturesque by-roads away from the mainstream of traffic, Adam had headed straight for the motorway. That would have brought them nearer to the end of the journey. As things were, he proposed spending the following night at Le Puy in the Auvergne, and arriving at the Villa des Roches the day after. Two more evenings in his company, Petra thought miserably. The strain was beginning to tell on her.

Dinner, however, passed pleasantly enough, with the children happily talkative now that their mother was recovering and would be joining them at their grandmother's house in three weeks' time. And that, Petra thought, will be where I bow out. She smiled at their chatter and felt a small pang. Children were so uncomplicated; what a pity all relationships weren't so straightforward.

Glancing up, she caught Adam's eyes upon her and had the curious sensation that he was reading her thoughts. He lifted the wine-bottle and refilled her glass without speaking.

After the children were in bed Petra made her telephone call to Di. She could visualise the tasteful little shop in the market-place, now quiet for the evening, with only the swifts and swallows weaving their tangled flights around the old buildings. Again she felt that cold sense of isolation and displacement. Once her place had been in that shop, and then—or so she'd thought—by Marcus's side. Now there was just . . . nothing. Mentally she shook herself. Melancholy achieved little; it only pulled you deeper into uncertainty. And the fact that Adam still hadn't raised the subject of Thomas's accident didn't help; that would come when the time was right. But in the meantime it hung over her like a sword of Damocles.

Deliberately she injected a note of brightness into her voice as she asked Di to organise some flowers for Unity. She was about to ring off when Di said tentatively, 'I suppose you wouldn't consider standing in for me at the shop when you come back? Just for a couple of weeks, Pet. I could take the opportunity to have a holiday, and I daren't leave Thea on her own—you know how scatty she is.'

Momentarily, Petra hesitated. Potpourri belonged to the past. She'd closed that particular book and hadn't intended to open it again. But Di was an old friend. And Thea would be there—frivolous, fun-loving Thea who, as Di's cousin, and recently back from South Africa, had jumped at the chance of buying out Petra's share in the business. All the same, Casterleigh again . . . And Marcus . . .

'All right,' she said slowly. 'Yes, yes, of course I will.'

'Oh, thanks. And by the way, Marcus was in the shop yesterday, asking for you,' Di said suddenly. 'I had the greatest pleasure in telling him grandly that you'd gone abroad for an unspecified length of time.

And that as you were travelling I had no idea how to get in touch with you. He looked a bit huffy. I don't think he believed me.' Di laughed. She'd never liked Marcus, despite his being the most eligible bachelor around Casterleigh, and her congratulations had been lukewarm when the engagement had been announced.

'What do you think he wanted?' Petra asked after a moment.

'Search me! I don't suppose he can really believe you've turned him down. Incidentally, how's it going with the great Adam Herrald?'

Petra attempted a laugh. 'Oh . . . fine. He's all right, I suppose,' she said lamely. There was no point in telling Di just what an ordeal this journey was turning out to be, and that at this very minute she felt like a schoolgirl, living nervously on borrowed time while waiting to be summoned to the headmistress's study.

'Only *all right?* A man like that! Oh, come on, Petra, he's got to be something more than merely all right.'

'Well, he . . . Look, Di, the last thing on my mind is a love affair, and I'd guess that's what you're hinting at. Well, forget it. He's not my type.'

'What type is he?' Di said mischievously.

'I wish I knew.' How would one describe Adam Herrald? As arrogant, overbearing, prejudiced? Or could she say that the children loved him, that he could be good company, and even perceptive and thoughtful at times? He was all of these things. The whole subject of Adam Herrald was far too complex to analyse in a short telephone conversation. 'Look, I've got to go, Di. You see to those flowers for me, and I'll see you get your holiday.' She replaced the receiver before Di could ask any more leading questions.

The dining-room was almost empty now. Adam had

announced that he was going to take a look around Moulins and would see them all at breakfast. 'Eight-fifteen,' he'd said, with a pointed glance in Petra's direction. Not so much an arrangement, she'd thought at the time, more a reminder that he gave the orders around here.

Aimlessly she went out to the little paved courtyard and ordered a pot of coffee. She sat watching the warm twilight deepen, the moths flattening themselves against the lighted window-panes. Somewhere a radio played a haunting Piaf song.

The conversation with Di had left her with a faint sense of foreboding. Marcus had been asking for her. Since she had broken off the engagement he had persisted in calling at her flat. He couldn't seem to get it into his head that she had really meant what she'd said that day . . .

They had been out riding and had gone into the house for a sherry. The house . . . Even here, its forbidding chill seemed to strike her; Cranbrook Place, a gothic pile built in the last century, since when nothing in it seemed to have changed. It was like a mausoleum for the Overton who had built it. And, on that sunny day, she had suggested a few changes she would like to make after they married.

Marcus's grey eyes had grown cold. And in the ensuing argument Petra had seen with chilly certainty that, after they were married, Marcus's mother would still be the mistress here and her own desires would count for little. Suddenly she had seen Marcus and Mrs Overton as allies against her—the newcomer. And that little glimpse into the future had shown her a lot of other things which she had overlooked. She awoke at midnight after that quarrel, her mind crystal clear, her brain resounding with a voice: *you can't marry him. You don't love him enough.*

The next day she had given him back his ring. And then had come his visits. Sometimes ridiculous, but always distressing. His tone had varied from patient disappointment to bitter recrimination.

And now she had committed herself to working in the shop again, if only for a couple of weeks during Di's holiday, back and visible within Marcus's orbit.

She shivered, then started, turning away quickly as Adam laid his jacket across her shoulders. 'I—I didn't hear you,' she began.

He glanced at the coffee-pot and said cryptically, 'Resigned yourself to a sleepless night, then?'

She was still trying to make the transition from the faintly depressing confusion of her thoughts to the present moment and the greater confusion of seeing Adam standing beside her, and she answered at random, 'I never sleep well in strange beds.' Then she flushed, guessing how he might interpret that remark.

'Really?' he said coldly. Then, after a moment, 'May I join you?'

'Am I in a position to say no?' She had recovered herself sufficiently to marshal her defences. He had come for his pound of flesh. Well, let's get it over and done with, she thought, sitting up straight. It's all I need to set the seal on a day that began to go wrong with his telephone conversation before breakfast.

In the gloom his face had hardened to a cold mask devoid of expression. He looked aloof, unapproachable. 'Of course you are,' he said icily. 'After all, I suppose you are off duty now. If you prefer to be alone, then so be it. I'm not begging, Miss Macey.'

Distractedly, she pushed back a wing of blonde hair. 'I apologise,' she said. 'I suppose that was rather rude. Please do sit down.'

She forced herself to look at him as she waited. The half-light sculpted the planes and hollows of his face firmly, and the strength she saw there made her shiver again, despite the covering of his jacket which held a faint, masculine fragrance that she found disturbingly intrusive.

'I hope that you're completely over your shock,' he said. 'I'm speaking of Thomas's adventure, of course.'

She sat back, shrinking into the warmth of silk-lined linen. 'Yes, I am. And so is Thomas. But something tells me that you're not going to allow me to forget it, are you? That's why you're here now.' She raised her chin a little. 'So you might as well let me have it with both barrels, and then perhaps——'

He shifted impatiently in his chair, his cigar glowing red. 'Are you always so much on the defensive?'

'Not always,' she said spikily. 'Only when I have to be.'

'I see.' His eyes narrowed to dark slits. 'And that means whenever we're alone together.'

'Are you surprised?' she flashed. 'After all, the first time we were alone you spent the whole of it putting me down. That seemed to set the pattern. And nothing that has happened since then has changed your opinion of me, has it?'

She wished that she could read his expression. Her words might have jogged his memory and reminded him of his opinion so forcibly expressed over the telephone to Jack Stansfield that very morning. And her remark might even give him a hint that she knew more than he thought; therefore he might, just *might*, feel a little guilty, a little ashamed.

But if he did, his face didn't show it. He merely said blandly, 'Oh, I don't know . . . I've noticed that you're quite good with the kids.'

'Thank you *so* much,' she blazed. 'It's a great relief to know that I'm not a hundred-per-cent failure. I'm glad that you've decided to upgrade me so that I now pass muster, despite all my faults.' She heard the biting note in her voice, but she couldn't suppress it. And why should she? Adam Herrald had the knack of bringing out the worst in her as a form of self-protection. No other man had affected her in this way before.

'Do you feel better?' he snapped. 'Now that you've got that off your chest?'

She glared at him. Why couldn't he leave her alone? She had felt edgy ever since that phone conversation with Di, and Adam's being here like this only strung her tension more tightly.

'Because if so,' he resumed, his voice flattening, 'we might even get around to having a normal, adult conversation. After all, in a sense this is part of the holiday, or, at least, an experience of foreign travel. So can't you try to enjoy any aspect of it?'

She gave a tinkle of laughter. 'I could. In other company,' she added meaningly. 'But there's no point in pretending. You feel that you owe me a severe ticking-off. You couldn't give me it with Thomas there, could you? And after all you've said about putting on a good front for the children's sake, you decided to postpone it. So you've——'

'Chosen this moment?' he bit out. 'Sought you out so I can give you a thorough blasting? Like the outright monster that I am? Is that what you're saying? Oh, for heaven's sake, Miss Macey, you're getting tedious. I've already said you're good with the children. And that includes Thomas. Even when he falls into rivers. He's also been known to go into a field with a very large bull, and to investigate the contents of his father's tool chest. He's a boy, nothing more, nothing less. And short of chaining him to you there's nothing you can do about it. So for God's sake can't we bury that little incident?'

Petra bit her lip, eyeing him uncertainly. He was certainly unpredictable. But despite his words she didn't trust him one inch. He drew his cigar into a glow that lit the sensuous line of his mouth as he returned her gaze steadily.

'If you say so,' she answered grudgingly at last.

'Good. At least that's *some* progress.' She still watched him warily, seeing the beginnings of that attractive, slightly crooked smile that could transform the harsh mould of his face. 'We might as well celebrate the truce with a nightcap. A liqueur and more coffee, perhaps?' The dark eyebrows rose enquiringly.

'I've already drunk three glasses of wine which you practically forced upon me,' she began, swallowing down a slight, fluttering breathlessness in her throat. 'So I don't think——'

'You were looking rather miserable,' he said offhandedly. 'You're not homesick, surely?' He half turned and gave the order to a hovering waiter.

'Heavens, no! Home is the last place I would——' She stopped. No point in resurrecting all that. And Adam Herrald was the last person to confide in. Besides, she needed all her wits about her to cope with this situation of merely sitting here with him in a soft dusk that had suddenly lost its tranquillity. The bleak, black side of Adam Herrald had frustrated and infuriated her. But his lighter side was equally deadly—perhaps more so. A velvet trap that would show its teeth of steel only after it was sprung.

'Good,' he said, 'because you're a long way from Casterleigh now.' He leaned forward, resting his elbows on the table, and she was irrationally aware of the breadth of his shoulders, the strong curve of his throat. 'Petra . . .' he murmured thoughtfully. 'It's an unusual name, and quite charming.' His gaze flickered over her warm face and moved up to rest on her pale, silky hair.

Resolutely she took a grip on the flutter that seemed to be spreading through her. Good heavens, she thought derisively, surely I'm not the kind of woman who goes soft simply because a man speaks to her pleasantly, and looks at her in a way that . . .? 'It was my mother's choice,' she murmured. 'She had always wanted to see Petra—the place. That poem, you know . . . It held a fascination for her. The "rose-red city——" '

' "—half as old as time," ' Adam finished.

She nodded. 'I don't think she ever expected to actually go there, so——' she shrugged '—perhaps she felt that the next best thing would be to give me its name.'

'And *did* she ever go?' Adam sat back idly as the waiter placed their drinks on the table.

Petra hesitated for a moment, then said, 'Yes. But . . . she was ill. Only my father knew how seriously. So he took her there—before she died.' Petra swallowed, wondering why on earth she had confided something which was so personal and still painful.

'I'm sorry.' Adam paused, then said, 'I hope it lived up to her expectations.'

'Yes, I believe it did,' Petra said in a low voice.

'Then in that, at least, she was fortunate. Reality has a nasty habit of falling far short of one's expectations sometimes.' A cynical note soured his voice, and Petra was silent, not knowing what to say.

He had once been married; perhaps that explained his remark, she thought. Maybe he was still smarting from a bad experience, a love dream that had turned into a nightmare.

She steered the conversation back into a less sensitive area. 'That left just my father and myself. He married again three years ago and now lives in New Zealand,' she added matter-of-factly.

'So you're alone,' he said casually.

She nodded. 'I was engaged, but not any more.'

'I had guessed as much.' Adam leaned across and picked up her left hand, gently stroking her ring finger with the tip of his thumb.

Recent thoughts of her mother had softened the shell which armoured Petra against him, and now the sensation of his touch on her skin lit a thousand lights that ran swiftly through her, as if her body were a pinball machine. In sudden alarm she pulled her hand away and saw his mouth twist briefly. 'So when this job's over what are you going to do?' he said after a moment.

With an effort she dragged her composure back and told him of her arrangement with Di. 'Then afterwards I might go to New Zealand. I don't know. It depends on—things.' She turned the conversation quickly away from her own uncertain future and said abruptly, 'What's Mrs Herrald like?'

For a moment his face closed thunderously against her as if her question was an impertinence. Then he gave a tight smile and relaxed. 'Oh, you mean—my mother? The children's grandmother? It sounded strange, for we all call her Venetia.' He lifted his cup. 'You'll like her, I expect,' he said casually, 'although you might have to make allowances for slight eccentricities. She's writing a book about the Ardèche area.

She's lived there for about ten years now, and so far not too many travel writers seem to have discovered it. I'm doing the photographs for the book, so this will be a kind of busman's holiday for me.'

Petra nodded. 'I see.' She hadn't met any writers, and she had a fleeting picture of an elderly, wispy-haired lady in ink-stained tweeds, pleasantly vague but rather trying.

'You needn't look so apprehensive. Venetia's fun, if a mite exasperating at times. But then, that's a Herrald trait, or so I'm told.' He lifted a quizzical eyebrow.

Petra looked at him, her slightly curving lips pronouncing silent agreement, and he smiled. 'And I think you'll like the villa,' he resumed, after a moment. 'Ruoms is the nearest small town—little more than a village, really, but lively enough during the summer. So providing you don't hanker after bright lights and casinos, I should think you'll be quite happy. And, of course, there are several interesting places within easy reach.'

'Sounds good,' she murmured, idly twisting her glass.

'And you can swim in the Ardèche river, although the villa has its own pool.'

'Then it's a good thing I packed a bikini.' Suddenly Petra laughed; the prospect before her seemed more inviting now. Even the aftermath of Adam's baffling early-morning telephone conversation had receded. It seemed a long time ago. She wondered if he felt that he had been too hard on her and was now trying to make amends by putting her at her ease. She ought to accept the truce, she told herself, for he could be very, very likeable when he chose to be. And that, together with his looks, could be quite a lethal combination to anyone who was susceptible. However, she reaffirmed silently, that didn't apply to her; as she had told Di, a love affair was right outside her brief. She simply wasn't interested. The upset with Marcus had shown her just how unreliable her own judgement could be.

Adam drained his glass then tilted his wrist to glance at his watch, and Petra stood up suddenly. 'I had no idea it was so late,' she murmured.

'I'll walk you across to your room,' he offered. 'It was quite enterprising of them to convert the stable block into an overflow annexe. Shall we go?'

'Oh, it isn't really necessary,' she demurred, prompted by a sudden need to get away from him. Their conversation had become dangerously close to intimacy once or twice, and that was something which a small inner voice warned her should be avoided; Adam Herrald would be a hard man to handle.

The impressions of the day tumbled through her mind like fragments of colour in a kaleidoscope, leaving her feeling suddenly disorientated and uneasy. Simply as the result of sitting opposite him and, for once, talking amiably, she felt herself to be vulnerable. She suspected that he might have deliberately engineered this; she didn't know him, and perhaps she never would. And she couldn't trust him. 'I'll go alone,' she said crisply. 'It's only a few steps.'

'Nonsense. You're not—afraid of me, are you?'

She pretended that she hadn't heard him, and as he draped his jacket more closely around her she hoped that he hadn't felt her slight quiver of apprehension.

She opened her mouth to protest again, then closed it. It would only look as if she was making a production out of a conventional courtesy. But was it just that? A hollow seemed to be opening up where her stomach should be, and she felt sudden panic as he took her arm. That traitorous tingle pulsed through her blood again. Walking close to him, the length of his body against her side brushed her lightly as they walked. Sheer maleness emanated from him with a force that couldn't be ignored. Every nerve in her seemed to signal its awareness of him. And she didn't want him! Didn't want any man! But least of all *him*. If Marcus had been the frying pan, then Adam Herrald was most surely the fire. This was simply a job, she reminded herself vehemently, trying to regain her composure. And her words to Di about romance had been the greatest truth she had ever uttered.

'Well,' she said with a tiny laugh, 'here's my room. We've arrived safely. So here's your jacket. Thank you for the loan, and . . . ' Her words faltered into silence as he drew her towards him.

One of his hands moved up to her face, cupping her chin and compelling her gaze. Helplessly she stared up at the blackness of his own. So *this* was his motive. Three glasses of wine, a liqueur, disarming conversation . . .

All part of the set-up; she had merely wondered and suspected when she should have *known*. Was it that he now saw in her a way of making this journey down through France more than a mere scenic trip?

She drew back sharply. 'Perhaps you didn't hear what I said this morning,' she snapped. 'I don't like being——'

Her words died as she stared up at him. His face was suffused with a cold, bitter rage. 'Shut up,' he gritted. 'Ah, for God's sake, shut up, Petra.'

She tried to wrench herself away from him, but he

held her in a cruel, bruising grip. Then his lips swooped down on to her half-opened mouth as powerful hands crushed her to him in an urgent spasm of power. The kiss was deep; it went on and on in total domination of her until her senses swung crazily. The stars receded, the buildings faded, and there was nothing in the world but the warmth of his body against hers, and the mastery of his hands, the passion that his lips spoke silently against her mouth. All her resistance had fled, eclipsed by a hunger that met and matched his own.

She heard him groan, a sound that seemed torn from him out of an infinite inner pain. Then his lips left her mouth and moved down to her neck, branding her from her ear to the hollow of her throat. Her hands were above his nape, her fingers avid and seeking in the dark, cool thickness of his hair. 'We can't stay here,' he said huskily at last. 'Come to my room.'

She sprang back, her eyes wide, desire quenched completely by the banal, over-used invitation. 'So that's it,' she spat. 'I *had* wondered if there was an ulterior motive behind your pleasantness this evening. Now I know why——'

'Why what?' he clipped out.

'Why you set up this scene, of course. We had all the trimmings tonight, didn't we? The softening-up process. And you thought I had fallen for it. What's the matter, Mr Herrald? Can't you bear to pass up an opportunity? Is our journey so dull that you have to try to inject a bit of excitement into it? Oh, don't bother answering,' she went on disgustedly. 'I simply don't want to know.'

'Come here.' There was an ominous threat in his voice.

She managed a short, derisive laugh. 'Didn't you hear what I said?'

'Oh, I heard, all right.' His hand shot out, his fingers gripping her upper arm. He swung her round so roughly that the heel of her shoe caught the edge of an uneven cobblestone and she stumbled, almost falling. But his hand held her, and instantly his other arm was around her. She was taken in a vice-like grip from which there was no escape. His mouth came down again in a lightning strike she couldn't evade. There was a burning savagery in his lips, a plundering strength that punished. Then, just as suddenly, he let her go.

She stared up at him, speechless with fury. His eyes were narrowed; there was no light in them, only a sombre, impenetrable blackness that hid his thoughts. But his mouth was a hard twist of contempt, and in it she saw ruthlessness, and an intent to take—if not by persuasion, then by force.

'Good*night*,' she whispered, her lip curling. 'Do I have to say it again? I object to being manhandled.'

'A great pity,' he murmured. 'You manhandle beautifully, Petra. Such a waste.' Then his voice sharpened. 'But don't pretend you're surprised that I kissed you. Surely, wasn't that part of the plan?'

'I don't know what you're talking about,' she snapped. 'If you think I deliberately——' She broke off, too angry for words, and stepped back, lifting one arm. For a second she savoured with immense satisfaction the prospect of feeling her hand connect with that brooding, bitter face. But he raised his hand, neatly deflecting her blow. 'Careful, Petra,' he grated. 'I don't take kindly to violence.'

'Except when *you* administer it,' she hissed. 'Well, get this, Mr Herrald. I have no plans to seduce you, strange as it might seem to you. Nor am I some naïve country girl ready to succumb to your macho attentions. I don't want them. Is that clear? It ought to be. But it seems you're the kind of man who thinks he's irresistible to women. But don't bank on it. *I* would say you—you're the vilest man I've ever met!'

She flung away, the jacket falling on to the cobbles, releasing again that whisper of masculine fragrance. He bent to pick it up, letting it trail negligently from his hand. 'Sleep well, Petra,' he purred. 'I expect you will. All this must have exhausted you.' His smile was a white, maddening glint in the darkness. 'Eight-fifteen tomorrow, remember?'

'I just wish to heaven I could forget!' She turned, forcing herself to walk composedly to her room. Everything in her cried out a need to run and hide from him, for ever.

As she closed the door to the old stable block she had a last sight of him, a pale glimmer in the darkness, and she thought she heard the soft note of laughter in the still night.

CHAPTER FOUR

PETRA couldn't get that second kiss out of her mind. Even as she removed her make-up, scrubbing at her lips as if to erase the fierce possession of his sensual mouth, she seemed to feel it again. A kiss like no other kiss she had ever known. Totally dominating, it had seemed to obliterate her as a person. It had been as if he had wanted to wipe her out.

But why? she wondered. She pummelled the pillow into an acceptable shape and lay, staring wide-eyed at the thin curtains stirring slightly in the night breeze. Could it be that, in spite of his dismissal of Thomas's accident, he had decided that she deserved some punishment? But did it have to be so extreme, so—bizarre?

She tossed restlessly. He had used the word 'psychotherapy' during his telephone conversation with Jack Stansfield, so might not that be the clue to his baffling behaviour? And did it all stem from his broken marriage? How little she knew about him! And how much better it would have been if she had thought to ask a few questions at the interview and at her meeting with his sister, Unity. Forewarned would have been forearmed.

But the main thing, she decided the next morning as she followed Sarah and Thomas across the courtyard, was to behave as if last night hadn't happened—or at least try to regard it as just one more pass by a man who couldn't resist asserting his male sexuality. All Adam Herrald deserved was contempt.

Her own response to his first kiss had been unpredictable, she remembered, her face growing hot. But that, at least, was understandable: the warm, starry night, the haunting music, the internal glow of three glasses of wine and a liqueur. And, of course, Adam's undeniable attraction and the faint aura of excitement which was always there, but, at certain moments, came across more potently.

But she wasn't going to give him the satisfaction of seeing her susceptibility. Nor would she walk into breakfast and behave in an uptight manner. That would only convince him that, one way or another, he had scored with her. And he hadn't!

A little tremor of apprehension shook her as she recalled that twisted white smile in the darkness, the sensation of his eyes upon her as she had walked away. And she stifled a sigh of relief on learning from the waiter that Adam and Patrick had breakfasted earlier and gone off into Moulins for half an hour. So perhaps, she told herself optimistically, he felt ashamed or embarrassed, and preferred to postpone the moment when they would again come face to face across the table. But then her common sense dismissed that thought; Adam was far too sophisticated and self-possessed to feel embarrassment over his actions. He probably hadn't given last night a second thought. And neither should she!

Petra knew from past experience that her cool, Nordic looks, her slim figure and the bandbox freshness which had become second nature to her sometimes offered a challenge which men found hard to resist. Smiling wanly, she broke her croissant; presumably some atavistic trait made them want to roughen and rouse her. 'An iceberg,' a man had once called her, disparagingly. But he had been quite wrong. She had known that she was as capable of passion as any other normal, healthy woman. It was all there, locked inside, waiting to be tapped. But at the right time. And by the right person, for the right reasons—which included love and respect, and she had never seen any point in pretending a response which she didn't feel, simply to satisfy a man's ego.

Marcus hadn't presented any problems in that department, she reflected. She had sometimes suspected that his sex drive was rather low, but had put it down to his sense of propriety and his ultra-conventional upbringing. Sometimes she had thought he showed more emotion over his horses than he did over her. And, after breaking off the engagement, she had wondered wryly if, for him, her attraction lay in the reputed stamp of breeding usually associated with fine-boned ankles and wrists and a slender neck.

She had even wondered if Marcus hoped that by mixing the Overton and Macey blood he would improve the Overton strain; a form of selective breeding which he profitably applied to the Cranbrook Place stables.

Still, she told herself, she was out of all that now.

She dabbed Thomas's mouth with a napkin and glanced up to see Adam approaching. His stride was leisurely, almost indolent, yet with that strange, tigerish grace she had noticed before. 'Good morning, Sarah,' he said pleasantly. 'And Thomas.' Then his voice lowered, his gaze lingered on Petra's face. 'Sleep well, Petra?'

Something in the way he spoke her name brought a shameful inner warmth. No longer 'Miss Macey'. 'Petra' now. A gate seemed to be closing, penning her in. But she managed to return his gaze coolly. 'Oddly enough, I did,' she said carelessly.

'Then perhaps it was that—nightcap we shared,' he said idly, but with a significance she chose to ignore.

'Perhaps it was. I must remember that Benedictine does the trick. Where's Patrick?'

'Already in the navigator's seat and rarin' to go.'

'Then we mustn't keep him waiting,' she said.

As Petra took her place in the back of the motor-caravan she had a vague sensation of having been let down in some indefinable way. Despite her own rationalising, she had half expected a sign from Adam making reference to her anger of the previous evening. And, although she had resolved to put it right out of her mind, it was a little humiliating to see that it hadn't made any impression at all upon him.

But soon her thoughts turned away from herself as the countryside of the Massif Central unfolded beyond the windows. About them lay a land of extinct volcanoes, forests, lush countryside away from the usual tourist routes. And then the skyline of Le Puy came into view and she gasped, leaning forward.

Adam smiled and drew in to the side of the road. 'Yes, it's really something,' he said. Then he turned to call Sarah forward, putting an arm around her as she stood between him and Patrick. 'A brief lesson,' he began, 'and something to write about in those journals that Petra's so keen on.' Then he went on to speak of the ancient volcanoes, the cores of which still pierced the bowl in which lay the clustered grey stone and red roofs of the town. 'And that,' he said, pointing to a tiny building perched precariously, 'is the Chapel of Saint Michael of the Needle.'

'I can see why it's called a needle,' Petra murmured, for the rock on which the little church was built stood up like a finger, slim and breathtaking in the afternoon light. She listened to him speak of the cathedral and its treasures, and stared about her, her hazel eyes wide. 'It's—unforgettable,' she breathed.

'We'll have some time to look around,' Adam said, putting the camper into gear when Sarah was safely in her seat again. Petra remembered then that this was where they were to spend the night. And this time, she decided firmly, she would go up to her room when the children went to bed. There wouldn't be even the remotest possibility of a recurrence of the previous evening's scene.

Later, as they visited the cathedral and stared at the rich vestments of the Black Virgin, she kept well away from Adam. And afterwards, as they wandered out through narrow, pedestrianised streets, gaily decked and fairy-lit for the town's festival, Petra walked with Sarah behind the others. Then Patrick grew bored. 'I'd like to climb up to that little chapel like the pilgrims did,' he said, slanting his eyes against the sun and staring up towards the tiny grey building.

'They probably crawled up on their knees,' Adam said, grinning. 'I doubt if your jeans would stand it.'

Patrick laughed. 'I mean I want to walk up, of course. I bet I could see for miles with my telescope.'

Adam glanced at Petra, his smile turning to half-mockery. 'Two hundred and sixty-seven steps carved out of the rock,' he murmured. 'Think you can manage it?'

'Certainly. I'm still sound in wind and limb,' she said loftily.

He laughed, and his gaze brooded slowly over her like a shadow, strangely chilling. 'Oh, you are,' he said softly. 'You most certainly are.'

'Well, then, let's go,' she snapped, turning away

quickly before he could notice her blush. He had been right when he spoke of her being on the defensive, she admitted to herself crossly; no other man had ever made her feel so mentally and emotionally vulnerable.

But only one more day, she reminded herself; there was a lot of comfort in the thought that tomorrow at this time they would be nearing the end of a journey where every hour seemed to bring its own particular problem. And after tomorrow there would be nothing to upset her, for she wouldn't be thrust into Adam's company for almost every waking minute.

The steps were easy enough, even for Thomas's short legs, and as they wound up the needle of rock the panorama of the countryside unrolled below them. The thin soil of the volcanic cone was studded with bright yellow stonecrop, fragile harebells and vivid poppies. Butterflies visited and rested, wings closed, and Sarah pulled Petra to frequent stops, delight hushing her voice to reverent wonder.

Petra felt the sun warm on her face, watched it gild Adam's nape as she followed him up. Her mood had swung again, and with the prospect of only one more day in his company she felt more carefree and relaxed than at any time since she had first met him at the ferry terminal. And, anyway, so long as his concentration was focused upon the children, as it was now, she could cope. She even found herself laughing at his infectious humour, listening with interest to his fund of information.

But of course, she warned herself, it was precisely at these moments that he was at his most dangerous. For, once having disarmed her, one sidelong glance of those dark eyes, a lift of that mobile mouth, and despite herself her composure would be threatened. And at such moments she had an awakening sense of being too much a woman. It was as if, at a stroke, he had the power to reveal depths of female sexuality in herself which she hadn't been aware of. It defied all logic, she thought, plodding upwards. For *any* kind of romantic attachment—let alone the travesty of romance and the lust which was what Adam seemed to be half offering—was the very last thing she needed.

But just now, in the golden afternoon sunshine, treading this ancient path and looking over the wall to the narrow river winding like a thread through little gardens below, there was no room for such complex thoughts.

In the tiny, dark church at the summit, Adam spoke quietly about its history, drawing her attention to the almost obliterated frescoes. In the gloom Petra noticed the play of light and shadow on his face and throat as he talked, listened to the deep, still timbre of his voice, saw the graceful, effortless way he turned and bent to lift Thomas. And suddenly, for no reason, the memory of that bitter, bruising kiss flooded back. She sensed again the strange, keen anguish in his momentary desire for her, felt again her own instinctive fear. And it seemed to spread into this moment so that even here, in this cool, peaceful place, the same panic possessed her. She shivered and turned quickly to the doorway, then found a seat in the sunlight outside. She sat gazing at the green-grey and saffron-coloured splashes of lichen on the stones, desperately willing calmness to return.

When Adam and the children joined her a few mintues later she was leaning back with her eyes closed, apparently basking in the sun.

'Had enough of mediaeval monuments?' Adam asked.

'I just needed to sit down,' she said tightly.

'But you are all right?' His indifferent tone told her that the question was put more out of politeness than concern.

'Yes, of course. Blame it on the steps.'

'I'm thirsty,' Thomas said hopefully, looking from Petra to Adam.

Adam laughed. 'All right, I can take a hint. Isn't that right, Petra?' His smile had hardened into a taunting curve. His meaning was clear to her, and Petra stared back at him, the gold flecks lighting her eyes.

'I hope so,' she murmured, and was disconcerted when Adam threw back his head and laughed.

She turned away quickly, flushing at his amusement. One more day, she thought with clenched teeth. I can stand anything—even him—so long as there's an end in sight.

They found a pavement café where the children could write the postcards they had bought at a stall by the foot of the steps.

Petra printed out a message in pencil for Thomas to ink over, and she was encouraging him gently, trying to put Adam's taunt out of her mind and recover her earlier calm. But she was aware that he was watching her, an infuriating half-smile lighting his face, and she found his scrutiny inhibiting. It was almost as if he guessed the effect that his gaze had upon her, and intended to exploit it to the full simply for the pleasure of making her feel uncomfortable.

So there was a sensation of release when a high voice behind her exclaimed, 'Why, Adam Herrald, of all people! I don't believe it! What on earth are *you* doing here?'

Startled, but relieved by the diversion, Petra

glanced up to see Adam rising quickly. 'Caroline! This *is* a surprise.' He was smiling easily, his dark eyes frankly curious. 'I might ask you the same question!'

There was nothing lacking in the warmth of *this* welcome, Petra thought drily, her mind going back to her first meeting with him. What a contrast!

The willowy brunette lifted her face to him, then with a slow movement, at once graceful and provocative, she raised a red-tipped hand and removed her sunglasses. She gazed at Adam with obliquely set eyes of an intense blue. 'I've been doing a spot of television work,' she murmured. 'So terribly exacting, and I'm completely exhausted. Then Teddie—you know Teddie Webster, darling—picked up a tummy bug and decided to fly home. So he lent me his car.' She sank down into the chair which Adam had drawn up for her. 'Oh, thank you.' She gave him the full benefit of her remarkable eyes.

'So you're seeing the sights of Le Puy?'

Caroline lifted one shoulder slightly. 'No, not really. It's not quite my kind of place. Actually, I'm on my way to Fréjus, to a friend's villa.' Then her gaze moved amusedly over the children and came to rest on Petra.

'You'll have a drink with us, of course,' Adam said, sitting down again and lifting a negligent finger towards a passing waiter.

Caroline gave a luxurious sigh. 'A *citron pressé* would be heaven,' she breathed. 'But you still haven't told me what you're doing here.' Her eyes considered the children again, and they returned her stare with slight belligerence. 'It looks like some kind of—outing.' Her laughter tinkled out.

'Hardly,' Adam said. 'But I haven't introduced you. Caroline Benton. Petra Macey. And my sister's children, Patrick, Sarah and young Thomas.'

'How cosy,' Caroline murmured.

'And Petra and I are taking them down to stay with their grandmother.'

'Lovely,' Caroline murmured politely.

She wasn't beautiful, Petra decided; she had something more vivid than mere beauty. She was . . . *arresting*. Thin, almost to the point of emaciation, she had a fragile, spun-glass elegance. 'And where, exactly, is that?' she asked, lifting strong, straight eyebrows. Expressions played across her face like sunlight on water, giving it a thousand moods and all of them compelling.

'In the Ardèche country. A little place called Ruoms,' Adam told her.

Caroline gave her eloquent shrug again. 'I'm afraid I've never heard of it. But then, geography was never my strong point. Oh, *thank* you,' she purred, as Adam poured iced water from the carafe on to the lemon juice in her glass. 'And what will *you* be doing in—Ruoms?' she asked, turning to Petra.

'Looking after the children,' Petra answered. 'That's my job.'

'Really? A nanny?' Caroline smiled as if Petra's answer had satisfied her. 'I must say you don't *look* like a nanny.' Her gaze took in Petra's simple black linen dress which accentuated the ash-blonde hair.

'That was Adam's reaction, too.' Petra looked across at him and saw that he was watching her with an unmistakable glint in his eyes, a half-smile shaping his mouth into its attractive, crooked curve.

Caroline shrugged off the remark with a languorous ripple of her shoulders. 'I seem to have been driving for ever,' she said, turning to Adam. 'I simply must find a hotel and have a long, long soak.'

Her presence had had the effect of paralysing the children's conversation. Sarah was still staring at her, but Patrick was fiddling with his telescope, while Thomas was busily making a thick border of crosses round the edge of his postcard.

Petra knew that in a little while Patrick would be fidgeting and wanting to move on, and she somehow sensed that Adam was in no hurry for that.

Caroline put down her glass and, giving Adam the full battery of her eyes, said, 'But *you're* not a nanny. And *you* won't be looking after the children.' There was an enticing tease in her voice.

'Officially, no. I'll be taking photographs.'

'Why not take them in Fréjus? Join me there. You know Tom and Patti Lorrimer, don't you? They'd love to have you, I know. There'll be quite a crowd of us, with nothing to do but soak up the sun and have fun.'

'It sounds great,' Adam murmured, smiling.

'And I'm sure you could do with a little fun, especially after so——'

'Well, I don't know about that,' Adam put in quickly.

Sarah was staring at him incredulously, tugging at his arm. 'But you *said* you'd be coming to Granny's,' she implored. 'You *promised.*'

'Of course I did,' Adam told her gently. 'And so I shall.'

Petra stared down at her lap, her face expressionless. What a pity he wasn't able to accept Caroline's invitation, she thought.

Caroline made a little moue. 'My loss,' she said lightly. 'I'll be there for three weeks or so, so if you do change your mind you know where to find me. And by the way, have you seen Leo Faulkner lately? Oh,

Adam, I simply must tell you . . .' She was leaning towards Adam, creating an intimacy that excluded the others, and her voice had dropped to a confidential murmur.

Petra stood up abruptly. 'Shall we find a post office?' she said, taking Thomas's hand. 'Back in ten minutes,' she mouthed as Adam glanced up and nodded.

The other two children joined her and they walked away, leaving Adam to what promised to be a very spicy morsel of gossip.

'You don't think he'll being her to *our* hotel, do you?' Patrick grumbled. 'Because if he does it means we'll have to have her with us at dinner. Women spoil things.'

'Do they?' Petra smiled. 'So *that's* what you think of me!'

'You're different,' he said bluntly, then darted off to examine some fishing-rods propped up outside a shop.

They had turned back towards the café after posting the cards when Petra saw Adam steering Caroline across the road towards a silver-grey convertible. For a moment he stood looking down as she got into the driving seat. They appeared to be deep in conversation, then Caroline smiled meltingly at him and drove off.

'Well, at least it's the wrong way for *our* hotel,' Sarah remarked with satisfaction as they waited across the road for Adam to join them. 'So she won't be with us at dinner.'

That evening, when Petra took Sarah and Thomas down, Adam was waiting with an aperitif for her and grenadine for the children which they carefully carried away to a small table. Adam was wearing a lightweight suit over a taupe shirt and tan tie. He raised his glass to Petra, his eyes taking in her appearance. The sun had slightly deepened her tan and brought a touch of warm colour to her cheeks which heightened slightly as he regarded her.

'It was a lovely afternoon,' she said carefully at last. 'Thank you for showing us around. I should like to come back to this place some time.'

'Yes, it has that effect on some.' His tone was careless, almost dismissive. He glanced at his watch, put down his glass and said, 'I must go. Tonight you'll be pleased to hear that you're dining without me.'

Petra stared challengingly at him, her chin tilted. 'I expect we'll survive,' she said levelly. 'Do enjoy your evening.' She raised her glass, her eyes mocking him over the rim.

'Oh, I intend to. I've ordered the wine for your meal. And a Benedictine afterwards.' She was about to thank him, feeling that perhaps her manner towards him had been unnecessarily cool, when he said softly, 'And don't wait up for me tonight, Petra.'

'I—I had no intention of doing so,' she retorted. 'Do you really think that I hung around last night in the hope of seeing you?'

He gave her a long, assessing stare and she felt the hot blood rise into her face. 'Look here,' she began, 'I think——'

'Sorry, my dear,' he said suavely, 'but I really don't have time to listen your thoughts, intriguing though they might be. As I said, I must go.'

'Then good*night,*' she snapped, and watched him go, pausing for a moment to speak to the children on his way out.

'I expect he's meeting *her*—Caroline,' Sarah said,

as she tackled her grapefruit. 'But that seems a bit funny, 'cos once I heard Mummy say that Adam didn't——'

'Sarah,' Petra said gently, 'I don't think we should discuss Adam. He must have lots of friends, and if he wants to take a lady out to dinner, then——'

'But that's just *it,*' Sarah persisted. 'Mummy said he *didn't*——'

'Sarah?' Petra's voice was soft, but firm with a note of warning. Then she went on, 'After we've eaten you can write up your journals, then bed. Tomorrow you'll be seeing your grandmother, and I don't want her to see you looking tired; she'll think I haven't been doing my job properly.'

The children began to talk of the last time they were at the Villa des Roches, and Petra ate her meal silently. Whatever Adam chose to do was his own business, but there was no denying that the evening had gone a little flat.

She had felt a sense of reprieve to learn that he wouldn't be dining with them, yet on the tail of that had come a sense of anticlimax. This meal with only the children had been peaceful and pleasant, but it lacked the piquancy of his presence, the flashes of humour, the sensation of being fully alive—a condition which was necessary, if only to parry his thrusts.

Her thoughts moved forward to the following day. She hoped that Mrs Herrald would be easy to get along with. It would be good to have the company of another woman again. Petra couldn't count those brief moments with Caroline Benton. That hadn't been companionship, merely an opportunity for Caroline to size her up. Petra smothered a faint smile, wondering if Adam had seen what lay behind

Caroline's manner. For within two minutes of Caroline having joined them Petra had realised where the other girl's interest lay, and that was with Adam.

So perhaps, she thought, he'll have more luck tonight than he had last night. Then she deliberately pulled her thoughts away from him. 'Come along,' she said to the children, 'it's time to go up now.'

CHAPTER FIVE

AS THEY drove south-east the following morning, the countryside began to change, growing perceptibly more mediterranean under an intensely blue sky. Hawks and kites circled the sunshine-gilded rocks. Wild fig trees grew haphazardly from crevices, cottages were hung with wistaria and vines under crinkled orange roofs.

Petra sat soaking it up as the children grew more and more excited at the immediate prospect of seeing their grandmother again.

It was late afternoon when Adam turned the camper into the drive that ran up to the Villa des Roches. Beneath a foam of candy-pink oleander a door opened eagerly, and a woman came towards them, her hands outstretched. The children raced to her, all chattering at once. She laughed, made a warding-off gesture, then bent to hug them.

Then she straightened, looking at Adam and then at Petra. Just for a moment her wide smile faltered as her eyes widened. Then she said hurriedly, 'You—you're Miss Macey, of course.'

There was a faint note of surprise in her voice, and Petra could only conclude that, like Adam, Venetia Herrald had anticipated someone quite different from herself.

'I do hope the children have behaved themselves,' the older woman resumed quickly. 'Journeys usually make them rather fractious.'

'They've been perfect,' Petra reassured her, taking

the firm hand held out to her.

'Good.' Venetia lifted her face for Adam's kiss, then tucked her arm into his. 'It *is* good to see you all, in spite of the unfortunate circumstances. You're in your usual room, of course, Adam. Miss Macey and Sarah will share. You won't mind, will you?' She flashed Petra a friendly smile. 'And Thomas and Patrick are together in the end room. Oh, leave the luggage until later . . . You'll be wanting to freshen up. Then we'll have tea.' She laughed, turning to Petra again. 'You see? I simply can't shake off my English habits, particularly one so civilised as afternoon tea.'

She hurried them into the house, as if anxious to get them safely settled under one roof. 'It's been so long since the house was full. And I'm longing to hear the news. Unity telephoned me . . . She asked me to thank you for the flowers you had sent, Petra. I may call you Petra? Good. I'm Venetia. We don't stand on ceremony here. Unity will be writing to you herself.'

After tea Petra excused herself and went upstairs to unpack for herself and the children, leaving the family to their talk.

The villa was cool and spacious, perched high above the river, and the room that she and Sarah were to share was white-walled and simply furnished. Apricot-coloured curtains sprigged with white daisies matched the two bedspreads; a tiny, adjustable spotlamp had been placed on one of the bedside-tables, presumably for Petra to read by in bed without disturbing Sarah. It was a thoughtful touch, as were the flowers on the dressing-table, and they gave a small insight into the kindness of the children's grandmother.

Petra moved over to the window and looked down

on to a patio and the motionless blue-green water of the swimming pool. Over to the right was a tiny peach orchard, the fruit hanging like jewels among the leaves, while beyond the pool a sweep of grass led to a small acacia grove that gave a band of dark, cool shade. And beyond that, Venetia had told her, were the rocky cliffs through which the river had worn its deep, narrow slot. 'Not so deep just now, though,' Venetia had added. 'In fact, you can walk across to the other bank, we've had so little rain.'

Petra was relieved to find that Venetia was neither the remote, eccentric intellectual of her imagination, nor had she any of the girlish mannerisms or hypochondriacal tendencies of Marcus's mother.

The atmosphere during dinner was pleasant, the talk confined to topics in which Petra could join. However, she had no wish to intrude upon a family evening to which Venetia had so obviously looked forward, and afterwards she excused herself and went upstairs. In the little chintz-covered armchair she tried to read, but her eyelids kept drooping. She was attempting the first page of a paperback novel for the third time when there came a tap at the door.

She opened it to see Adam standing there, silhouetted against a lamp on the landing, the shape of his dark head rimmed with golden light. Instantly she was wide awake and wary.

'I've come to take you down,' he said, regarding her with narrowed, speculative eyes. 'Sorry, Petra, but you'll just have to deny yourself the luxury of solitude for a while longer.'

His tone stung. 'Is that a reproof?' she asked. 'Another way of reminding me that I'm still on duty?'

'Not at all, but if you choose to take it that way . . .'

He shrugged.

'And just for the record, I wasn't indulging a wish for solitude. I simply thought you would want to talk family-talk.'

'Really?' There was a caustic note in the word.

'Yes, really,' she snapped. Her lethargy had gone. Adam Herrald had the effect of an ice-cold shower, stinging every fibre into instant reaction. Something about the sight of him leaning negligently against the door-jamb set her stomach lurching, and the carefully damped-down resentments of the journey sparked again in sharp protest.

'Then maybe I should point out, just in case you hadn't noticed,' he said coldly, 'that I was born into a family hospitable enough to include whoever else happens to be around at any given moment.'

'Really?' she said, mimicking the acid tone, the barely moving lips. 'Now you *do* surprise me. You're one of the family, yet I would have said that the word was definitely *inhospitable.*'

He regarded her in silence for a moment, then continuing in a bored voice which dismissed her remark as unworthy of his comment, drawled, 'So for the time being you had better count yourself as one of the family.'

Petra gave a short laugh. 'How invitingly you put it,' she murmured.

With an exasperated sigh he pushed one shoulder against the wall and straightened. His height and presence seemed to threaten like a giant wave, and she caught her breath, remembering the strength of that body as she had known it two nights ago. His voice rasped as he said, 'Oh, for heaven's sake, come along. Whether you like it or not, you're part of this family for the time being. It goes with the job, as you should know. So stop being so awkward at every blasted turn.'

'Awkward? How can you say that?' she flared. 'What do I have to do, for heaven's sake? Put up with all your rudeness, take whatever you choose to hand out without a murmur? You're living in a bygone age if that's what you expect from me.'

'I've stopped *expecting* anything from you,' he gritted. 'But I would like to point out that we're both guests in Venetia's home. Does that mean anything to you?' His hands came out and she backed away, but too late. His fingers clenched on her shoulders, and he gave her a little shake, as if to emphasise his words. 'Whatever your reason for taking this job, you're going to do it properly. And what applied on the journey still goes. Have you got that?' The glittering intensity of his eyes held her gaze. For a moment she felt weak, then she wrenched herself free of him.

'Are you trying to tell me—that I've still got to go on—being nice to you?' Her eyes blazed with a golden fire that met his own. 'Well, I only hope that I can manage it, because you make it almost impossible.'

'Oh, God,' he said from between clenched teeth, 'heaven preserve me from from self-opinionated blondes who——'

'And,' she cut in, raising her voice slightly, 'correct me if I'm wrong—and I'm sure you'll do that anyway—but somehow I had the impression that you would be going your own way once you had—how did you put it?—*offloaded* us.'

'As I fully intend to,' he snapped, 'when it suits my convenience. All right? Now, could you make a supreme effort and try to look pleasant? For the sake of the children and Venetia?' His fingers closed round her arm, jerking her round to face him. 'She's no fool, you know.'

'You don't have to tell me that,' Petra said sweetly. 'I've got eyes, haven't I? And let go of my arm. Or haven't you got the message yet?'

For a moment they stared at each other, the atmosphere between them ticking like a timebomb. Then he dropped her arm. 'Oh, I think I've got it all right. You enjoy games. You like to play hard to get. Certainly you've succeeded in entertaining me, although I could have done without it.'

'Hard to get?' Her voice was a whisper of incredulity. 'My goodness, I knew you were conceited, but I never dreamt that even *you* could be so utterly vain as to assume that I want to play any games at all with you!'

He didn't answer, and as he stared down at her she found her own gaze falling away. 'Well?' she said in a low, furious voice. '*Are* we going down? Isn't that why you're here? Or was it one more excuse to prove how objectionable you can be? Because, believe me, I don't need any more proof of *that!*'

She brushed by him, and without another word he turned and followed her down. She sensed his gaze on the back of her hair, and she straightened her shoulders, her head spinning. Her heart was hammering, and anger seemed to throb through every beat, exhausting her. And the strange thing was that she couldn't quite understand how it had all started, how his simple request should have led to their flinging insults at each other. Something in our respective chemistry, she decided wearily. He had been determined to dislike her from the very beginning, even before he had spoken one word to her. But if he thought she was going to let him trample all over her, then he could think again. Whatever lay behind his manner towards her—and presumably it was something to do with his broken marriage—didn't justify his hateful behaviour.

She blinked and moistened her lips, then, framing a careful smile, she joined the others in the cool, restful sitting-room, her anger only partly submerged.

But in the general relaxed atmosphere of friendliness and affection it would have been petty to let her own inner turmoil spoil the evening. After a while in the undemanding company of the children and their grandmother, Petra felt the tidal wave that Adam had set in motion flatten out.

'You have a lovely home, Mrs Herrald,' she said, looking around at the great jugs of flowers and the Van Gogh prints.

'Yes, I love it here. But you really must call me Venetia. Everyone over the age of eighteen does. And tomorrow I'll show you my garden. I'm proud of that, too. I take it that you like flowers?'

Petra nodded. 'Gardening, too,' she murmured. 'At home I've only a tiny plot. I concentrate on miniature plants, or those with tiny florets and leaves.' She went on to tell Venetia of her dried-flower work, finding an appreciative audience in the older woman.

After a while Venetia got up, smoothing down the blue shirt she wore over faultlessly cut matching slacks. Her hair was an unashamed dusty-grey, but beautifully coiffed; her skin was perfect, and above frank grey eyes her brows were clear and very dark, a lingering indication of the original colour of her hair. There was an understated elegance about her, Petra thought admiringly, as if she had easily mastered the French flair for making the most of one's appearance without resorting to unnecessary clutter.

'I'll do the dishes now,' Venetia murmured, then as Petra got up to help her she held up an admonitory hand. 'Alone, my dear. Actually, I quite enjoy it. During the day I have Monique to help in the house and prepare the evening meal. You'll be meeting her tomorrow, and her husband, Edouard. He does the garden, cleans the pool and takes care of any odd jobs around the place. Now, if you'll excuse me . . .' She beamed happily on them all and went out.

Patrick and Thomas were building a model car at a card table set up in the window, and Sarah threw down her comic and crossed to the boudoir grand piano in the corner of the large room. She lifted the lid, then fumblingly began to play a Chopin prelude. Adam winced as she hit the wrong notes then crashed her hands down in a loud discord. 'I'll never be able to do it,' she wailed. 'I've been on this piece for six weeks, and I so wanted to be note-perfect for when Daddy comes home.'

'I think we can fix that,' Petra said comfortingly, getting up. 'I'll help you, shall I?'

Adam raised quizzical eyebrows. 'Pressed flowers? Chopin preludes?' he murmured in velvet tones. 'Is there no limit to the talents of our estimable Miss Macey?'

Petra's head snapped up, her eyes narrowing, a retort ready upon her lips. Then she remembered the children and smothered it. Was there no end to his nastiness? She looked at him scathingly and rippled out an arpeggio, then she began to play the piece that Sarah had attempted.

The mellow tones of the old Bösendorfer filled the room with sweet, plaintive melody as Petra played with a gentleness that she was far from feeling. Then she moved on to a mazurka.

As the last strains died she found her gaze drawn towards Adam. He was sprawled in the deep, easy chair, his opened book face-down on the arm, his long length stretched out in an attitude of profound stillness, watching her through half-closed eyes. After a second he said softly, 'Bravo, Petra. I hope you'll favour us with more recitals.'

She regarded him coolly. 'Maybe I will—*if* you're here,' she said pointedly.

'Oh, I shall make a point of it,' he drawled, smiling as her eyes narrowed.

'Now that was delightful,' Venetia said, coming into the room with a dishcloth in her hand. 'The piano hasn't been played like that since Adam's father died. I keep it tuned, of course, but . . .' She shrugged ruefully. 'Patrick—my husband, Patrick, that is—bought it during our first year of marriage. You must feel free to play whenever you like, my dear.'

'Petra's going to help me,' Sarah put in.

'That's fine. But not tonight, I think.' Venetia glanced at the little ormolu clock on the bureau. 'It's way past your bedtime, darling. And I'm sure we're all tired. Oh, and Adam, after I've taken Petra round the garden tomorrow I'd like to run over my book with you, then perhaps we can talk about the illustrations?'

Petra had risen, picking up Thomas's blue elephant in one hand, and holding out the other towards him. His eyes were sleepy and heavy-lidded. 'Carry me,' he pleaded.

'You're just a big baby,' she teased, then bent to pick him up. In straightening, she met Adam's eyes again. Their expression was unfathomable; his face wore the stony anonymity of their first meeting. 'Goodnight,' she said after a moment, her lips shaping the word stiffly, then she went out, followed by Sarah and Patrick.

She awoke the following morning to hear sounds from the pool below, and she opened the window to see Adam cutting a slow, lazy crawl through the water. She leaned out, breathing deeply. The air smelled of herbs and growth. Lifting her head she could see traffic crossing the short bridge to the little town on the opposite bank, the huddle of glowing roofs, the cream and ochre buildings. Already the sun was warm. Behind her, Sarah still slept.

Adam reached the end of the pool, shook the water from his hair, and glanced up. 'Come on in,' he called softly.

Petra shook her head. 'The children——' she mouthed.

'What harm can come to them?' he said indifferently. He hoisted himself out of the pool and stood with the bright water dripping from him. Then he dived, cleaving the water with hardly a splash.

For a while she watched him, hypnotised by the fluid motion of his brown body in the blue-green water. It looked inviting. And she wouldn't have to actually talk to him . . . Their argument of the previous evening had drained her, and she had resolved that her best policy was to ignore him as far as she could, to stay cool and not give him the satisfaction of seeing that, by a few calculated remarks, he could succeed in getting under her skin. That, perhaps, had been the whole trouble: he sensed that she was vulnerable, and he couldn't resist demonstrating his power over her.

Not any more, though, she told herself doggedly, as she pulled on her bikini.

'I'm not in your league,' she said as she joined him.

After her first glance at him she looked carefully away from the smooth brown skin that gleamed in the sunlight, and the dark triangle of hair that furred his chest, trapping drops of water like diamond chips.

'Oh, I don't know . . . You're not so bad,' he said with a glint in his eyes as his glance slipped over her.

She opened her mouth, then determinedly closed it. She would *not* rise to his taunts. But under his gaze her body seemed infused with shimmering life, as if that dark stare generated a new, vibrant energy in her. She took a deep breath and jumped, then gasped at the shock.

His husky laughter reached her. 'Softie,' he murmured. 'It'll warm up in an hour or so. Well, *swim*, girl. Don't just shiver. Here, come on.' He took her hands and, lying on his back, drew her along the pool to the deep end. 'There,' he said, his hands clipping her bare waist firmly as he held her up. She gripped the rim of the pool, treading water, and his hands fell away as if her body was no more than a parcel he had delivered safely.

She hung there, watching him. He moved like some aquatic animal, perfectly at home in its element, and apparently unaware of her now. 'Well, *good*,' she murmured softly. Perhaps he had got the message at last.

She swam for a while, then got out. Adam joined her, draping a big, fluffy towel around her shoulders. 'Enjoy it?' he asked carelessly.

She nodded. She felt uncomfortably exposed and moved away. 'Very much,' she said shortly.

'Perhaps we should do it often,' he suggested in silky tones. 'How about meeting early every morning

—a clandestine swim before breakfast?' There was a suggestive challenge in his eyes, a lurking mockery in the sensuous twist of his smile. His tanned body revealed his muscles in strong and rounded beauty. She felt an almost uncontrollable urge to touch him, and was horrified at herself. She pulled the towel more closely around her, turning away quickly. 'Every morning?' she muttered negligently over her shoulder. 'Surely you won't be here *every* morning—will you?' She buried her face in the towel, conscious of a need to hide from him.

'Now there you go again,' he said lazily. 'You still haven't got it right, Petra. An intelligent girl like you! I shall be out during the day working, that is if Venetia's ever going to get her book off the ground.' He pulled the towel from her face, and she stared up into his eyes for a moment. 'But I shall definitely be here every morning. Sorry to disappoint you.' His smile was deliberately challenging now as his eyes raked her body with undisguised admiration. 'What's the matter? Afraid of me? Still?'

'Certainly not,' she retorted hotly, then made an effort to calm herself as she began to towel her hair. 'It's just that you're not my flavour of the month. Did you expect to be?'

'How can I say,' he murmured with infuriating smoothness, 'not knowing your particular tastes?'

'Look,' she said, beginning to feel that she was as much out of her depth here as she had been in the water, 'let's not start all that again. I don't——'

'Just as you say,' he said softly. But she knew that he was laughing at her, and that he had perceived that she wasn't as cool as she had intended to be.

Damn him, she thought, as she dressed quickly in the bedroom. Why should she be preoccupied by him? Because, she answered herelf, he was impossible to ignore, of course. One couldn't help but be aware of him; he was so—so *vital*. The kind of man who could enter a room and you would know he was there, even before you turned and saw him.

And she was here to work, she reminded herself vehemently, slipping her feet into striped mules. This job was a bolt-hole, an escape from Casterleigh and Marcus's importunings. A place where she could get herself together and work out her future. She didn't need the distraction of Adam Herrald's baffling, mercurial moods, his monumental egotism. There was no room in her life for a man, she reiterated silently. Not for *any* man, not at this moment. But in particular, not a man like Adam Herrald, more at home in the sophisticated world of women like Caroline Benton who, no doubt, would have been able to take all this in her stride.

Adam spent the morning closeted with Venetia in her study, and when, in the afternoon, he checked his camera equipment and drove away, Petra breathed a sigh of relief. The house seemed a more tranquil place when he was out of it.

As the days went by Petra gradually slipped into a gentle routine, swimming in the pool with the children, or down below in the clear river, which ran shallow and narrow and perfectly safe between the rocky escarpments. She stayed away from the pool before breakfast and assiduously avoided being alone with Adam. And for a time she relaxed in the undemanding pattern of the long, warm days.

Each morning after breakfast Venetia shut herself away in her study, and sometimes Petra would take Sarah and Thomas off into the town for ice-creams, or wander through the market under the avenue of trees, pausing to buy herbs or sausage, and to examine the bright plastic toys which captured Thomas's interest. Often Thomas was allowed to 'help' Monique in the kitchen, while Petra devoted her time to improving Sarah's playing. Patrick was conspicuous by his absence, for he had picked up the threads of an earlier friendship with Marcel, a local boy who spoke good English, and they followed their own devices.

Occasionally Adam was around, developing film in the tiny dark-room he had set up in the cellar, sometimes lounging by the pool. But most mornings he drove away in the camper, to arrive back in the evening in time for pre-dinner drinks on the patio. And gradually, almost without becoming aware of it, Petra found herself watching the clock for that hour, against all conscious will looking forward to his return. His manner might be unpredictable, his remarks to her sometimes barbed in a way that only she could recognise, but he was never boring, she decided. Like the spice that sharpened a bland, agreeable dish, he added an indefinable but positive excitement.

She watched the children respond affectionately to him, noted that Venetia's laugh rang out more frequently when he was there, and dimly Petra sensed that, because they were all together, the evening became the best part of each day.

After the children were in bed, and Venetia had asked Petra to play for them one evening, she put down her tapestry and said suddenly, 'Adam, I think it's high time we gave Petra a day off.'

'Quite right,' Adam said equably. 'You're probably infringing all kinds of labour rules working her like a slave as you're doing.'

Petra laughed. 'Who's complaining?' she said lightly, her fingers moving into a Debussy composition. She was hardly listening, her mind relaxed by the slow tempo of the music, the sense of physical well-being which had grown over the past days. Then, with sudden shock, she heard Venetia say, 'So why don't you take her out for the day, Adam? Show her some sights.' She turned to Petra. 'It would be a great pity, my dear, if you were to leave here without having been further than Ruoms market-place, don't you think?'

'Well, I . . . I hadn't really thought about it,' Petra said lamely, her thoughts in disarray. She stared at the reflection of her moving hands in the polished rosewood. The peace of the evening had been shattered by Venetia's suggestion as surely as if it were brittle glass. She couldn't look at Adam. 'And besides,' she hurried on, 'I'm sure Adam's too busy . . .' Her voice trailed away in embarrassment.

'No,' he said thoughtfully, after a pause. 'I'm not *too* busy. And Venetia's right. It's time you broke free of those kids for a day. It might make a new woman of you.'

What on earth did he mean by that? Petra wondered. If they had been alone she would have demanded that he explain his remark. She bit her lip, then said, 'Really, Venetia, I'm all right. And I'm certainly not overworked,' she added weakly.

To be alone with Adam again . . . Her stomach seemed to shrink. And just when they had settled into a fairly normal routine, undisturbed by any open hostility between herself and Adam . . . She shot him a quick glance, but he was stubbing out his cigar, his head bent. Inwardly he must be furious at being inveigled into a position where he would have to devote a day to acting as her guide. Petra had sensed by his response that he wasn't in favour of the idea. But, of course, he had had no choice but to agree to Venetia's suggestion.

'And besides,' Venetia said decisively, taking up her canvas again, 'I, too, need a day off from my book. And I'd like to spend it with my grandchildren, naturally.'

'Then that's settled,' Adam said with finality. 'You're going to get your day off, Petra, even if the prospect horrifies you.'

'Oh, it does.' Petra gave a frivolous laugh for Venetia's benefit, but her words weren't so far from the truth. A whole day alone with Adam! It was the last thing she wanted.

Later, when Venetia had gone away to make a telephone call, Petra stared at Adam stonily. 'Look,' she said tartly, 'I realise that I'm being foisted upon you, and that you didn't have much say in the matter . . . But surely you can invent an excuse? Can't you be too busy, or something? If I must go sightseeing, then I can take a coach—or an excursion, I suppose? There's no need for *you* to be involved.'

The guarded expression of his face darkened as his strong brows locked and his mouth tautened. In a second, all the old enmity between them blazed again like a smouldering fire which needed only the smallest breath of wind to bring it into crackling flame.

'Venetia wouldn't hear of your going off on your own,' he said tersely. 'Can't you at least *appear* to appreciate her consideration, even if you don't?'

'I *do* appreciate it,' Petra sparked, her chin going up. 'Why do you deliberately misunderstand my motives? It's the kind of—generosity that's part of her. I'm well aware of that. But I——'

'Then for God's sake stop making a production out of it,' Adam bit out. 'I don't intend to ravish you in some ravine, if that's what's worrying you.' He watched her for a moment, his eyes narrowed and speculative. 'Or is this part of your tactics, too?'

'I don't know what you mean,' she retorted.

'Oh, I doubt that,' he murmured maddeningly. 'Still, leaving all that aside, I'll give you your day out. I'll show you sights you'll never forget. That's the object of the exercise. And *only* that,' he ground out. 'So stop being so obstructive, *whatever* your reasons.'

She locked her hands together in impotent fury. 'I am *not* being obstructive. Can't you understand that? It hasn't escaped my notice that the prospect of a day alone together is as unwelcome to you as it is to me. And surely you can conjure up an excuse that would, at least, postpone it.'

'You heard what Venetia said. She wants a day with her grandchildren. So—put off the evil day?' He laughed smokily, maddening her, and she heard a predatory amusement in the husky notes. 'No, my dear,' he went on creamily, 'if life has taught me one thing, it's that nothing is improved by deferring the moment, as if it might go away. It won't, Petra. It seems we're going to be stuck with each other. So,' he resumed, his voice taking on a conversational tone as Venetia's step was heard outside the door, 'we'll make an early start and get a few miles behind us while the day's still cool.'

Frustrated, a sense of dread welling up in her, Petra could only murmur her agreement as she turned back to the piano.

CHAPTER SIX

SOON after eight o'clock on Thursday morning, Petra climbed into the passenger seat of the motor caravan. She had slept badly, apprehensive of the day ahead. Her misgivings had deepened as she dressed, apathetically choosing a green and white lawn dress—the coolest thing in her limited wardrobe.

Now, as she smoothed it over her knees, Adam engaged the gears, giving her a quizzical glance as if he could read her thoughts. Then he said idly, 'You look like a salad, Petra. Very refreshing.' A faint smile hovered on his mouth as they turned out into the road.

'Do I?' she said tightly. 'Is that meant to be a compliment? If it is, then top marks for originality.'

He laughed. 'Yes,' he nodded, 'a salad. Definitely. Cool and crisp. And straight from the fridge.'

She didn't answer. What was the point? Let him have the last word, she told herself. He was *not* going to goad her. But the day stretched before her like a perilous sea, troubled by uncharted depths, dangerous with undercurrents.

As if to aggravate matters, she was persistently aware of his closeness in the driving seat beside her, of his strong, brown hands on the wheel, the play of muscles in his long, taut thighs as he braked at the crossroads.

She turned to stare fixedly out of the window, desperately trying to distance herself into a state of mind that excluded him. This whole trip was ludicrous!

she thought. Two people who disliked each other, who, like flint and tinder, struck sparks almost every time they exchanged a word or glance when no one else was present. Yet here they were, thrust together for a day in a beautiful landscape. And all due to Venetia's thoughtfulness! With any other man but Adam it might have had a note of ironic humour. With him, it certainly was nothing to laugh at!

But Petra had reckoned without the breathtaking magnificence of the scenery. Insidiously her admiration and interest shredded away her intention to isolate herself from Adam's effect upon her, and as they drove to the start of the Ardèche gorge she gasped with delight. Adam made no comment but pulled into the first belvedere, and they got down from the camper to look at the river below, coiled like a slim, green snake, dappled with tiny, bright canoes.

'Well?' he murmured as she stared at the soaring span of the rock arch, hollowed out by thousands of years of floodwater. 'What do you think of that?'

She shook her head dazedly. 'It's—indescribable.'

'Of course, the best way to see the gorge is from down there, in a canoe. Now that's really something.' For a while they stood in silence, then he touched her arm. She stiffened involuntarily. 'Lots more to see,' he reminded her brusquely. 'We've got quite a day ahead, so we'd better start moving . . .'

It was a thrilling journey of hairpin bends and spectacular views. The road unreeled a vista of caves and chasms, cream and grey towering cliffs, awe-inspiring as cathedrals, and when Adam finally parked the camper and found a café by the river near St Martin Petra sank down on her chair with a sigh.

'I feel quite—bemused,' she murmured, then

laughed. 'A surfeit of splendour.' When Adam didn't speak, just sat watching her with a slight smile on his lips she glanced away, then said in a small voice, 'You were right. Already I've seen sights I'll never forget.' She put on her sunglasses, her mood changing as she recalled the acrimony behind that promise of his when the whole subject of this journey had been one more battleground.

She waited for him to make some remark which would reinforce the barrier between them, but he merely said, 'And the day's only half-way through.' He ordered ham sandwiches which came as vast, crusty rolls filled with generous shavings of tender, pink ham.

Petra sat quietly, watching groups of teenagers spilling out of vans stacked high with canoes. The festive atmosphere, the colour and gaiety in the sunshine was a scene to be treasured, she thought, to be brought out of memory and looked at during the long, grey English winters. But she wouldn't be in England . . . Would she? She pushed the question aside. Time enough to think of the future. Today there was only—*today*.

Much later, as they sat in the Jardin de la Fontaine in Nîmes, Petra surreptitiously slipped her feet out of her sandals and gave a contented sigh. 'What can I say?' she murmured. 'This has been a wonderful day. I can understand why Cézanne and Van Gogh loved this countryside.'

'Pity we can't include a trip to Arles and St Rémy,' Adam said. 'Maybe another day . . . And if we squeezed in Aix-en-Provence I would take you to Cézanne's studio where you could stand where he worked, and you'd swear that he had just popped out for a minute.'

'Perhaps that's how life is,' Petra sighed, lifting her face and feeling the sun's warmth on her closed eyelids. 'I mean—that we leave something of ourselves behind, in the places where we were happy or fulfilled. Maybe I shall leave a little of myself here.' She stopped, then hurried on, her voice flattening. 'Anyway, thank you for giving up your day just so that I could goggle and rubber-neck.'

'The pleasure's all mine,' Adam murmured.

She glanced at him sharply. 'Oh, I doubt that,' she said. 'You've seen it all before—probably several times. So you don't have to be polite. Not to me, remember?'

He laughed, and she tilted her head back again. 'All this is a bonus. Naturally I hadn't anticipated it. I'd expected to devote all my time to the children, inventing games for them, sort of keeping myself at their level of enjoyment.' She opened her eyes, and saw that he was watching her with concentrated attention. For once there was no cynical glint in his eyes, no disparagement in the sensual sweep of his mouth. It was almost as if he were listening or watching for a sign, a clue to some mystery. Then the expression vanished, and Petra wondered if she had imagined it.

'As I said,' he murmured, 'I, too, have enjoyed the day. And I wasn't being merely polite.'

His gaze held her own. She felt her face grow warm with a heat that had nothing to do with the sun, and she looked away quickly. 'Well, then, perhaps that's because you're interested in stone, rocks, old ruins. Aren't they your passion?'

'Among others,' he nodded, a teasing glint lightening his dark eyes. 'But how did you know?'

She shrugged. 'Something Venetia said.'

'She talks too much,' he said idly, but Petra felt that there was something guarded behind his words.

'No, not really. We weren't discussing you, if that's what you're thinking. It was just her answer to a remark I'd made about light and shade on the walls of the villa.'

'Light and shade,' he mused. 'Shadows and sunlight on old stone . . . And moonlight, too. Light is a tireless artist, the greatest of all. It never stops painting, transforming, tricking . . .'

'I think I know what you mean.' Petra leaned back again, closing her eyes, experiencing a strange sense of completeness. It was as if all the frayed ends had been spliced into a silky smooth cord that held them together in golden sunlight. Who would have thought it could be like this? she wondered. She had been so sure that long before the afternoon her nerves would have been jangled to the pitch where she could have screamed with the frustration he could so easily generate in her. It just didn't seem credible that this man who sat beside her now—who had answered all her questions so patiently, and in such an entertaining manner, this man who had deliberately put himself out to please her—was that same Adam Herrald whose black gaze could shrivel her, and whose bruising kiss had held a note of sadistic revenge. The haunting bitterness of that kiss flooded back, and she gave a little shiver which deepened as he moved, his bare forearm brushing hers for a moment.

'You know,' he said thoughtfully, 'you never did tell me why you took on this job. The more I see of you, the less it seems likely that you would——'

She grinned, relieved to turn her thoughts into another channel. 'It's not so very strange. The job just happened to be advertised at a time when I wanted to get away from Casterleigh for a while.'

'For any particular reason?'

'Oh, several,' she said lightly, deflecting his curiosity. She didn't want to talk about Casterleigh or Marcus or anything which would cast a shadow over this day. 'It's almost five,' she added quickly. 'Oughtn't we to be thinking about getting back?'

'If we must.' He took her arm as they walked back to the camper. The slight pressure of his long, cool fingers on her bare skin sent a tingle of melting, sensual pleasure through her veins. She stared about her, chattering with conscious vivacity to disguise the effect of his touch.

She knew that her feelings about him had undergone a subtle change during the day; now the emphasis lay not on the animosity he could arouse in her, but on the sheer magnetic attraction of him, and the kindness and sense of humour that were part of the make-up of this complex man. A week or so ago she had concluded that no woman in her right mind would be able to put up with him. But today she was seeing him in a different light. But that, too, had its dangers.

At Pont-St-Esprit he parked the camper and led her down a shabby little street. 'Now this isn't much of a restaurant,' he warned, opening a faded green door, 'but——' His words were lost as a middle-aged woman hurried forward with an exclamation of pleasure and held out her arms. Adam lifted her clear of the floor and kissed her firmly on both cheeks as she prattled with joy.

Petra couldn't understand the voluble French, but when she and Adam were seated at a plastic-covered table in a drab back-room, he explained. 'That's Jeanne. She used to work for Venetia, then she and her husband took over this little place from her mother. That's *maman*, over there.' He nodded towards a television set in the corner where a wrinkled, black-clad woman nursed a small white poodle, oblivious to everything but the picture before her.

Petra laughed. 'All that wonderful country out there, and here she sits watching something that's probably had at least three repeat showings. Or doesn't French television work that way?'

'I don't know.' Adam smiled. 'Still, it takes all kinds, you know. And I should warn you that this won't be gourmet fare, but I don't suppose you'll complain.'

'I wouldn't dare,' Petra grinned, her eyes sparkling.

The meal was simple. A puffy, melting omelette followed by the freshest trout Petra had ever tasted, and tender young green beans glistening with a delicate sauce. Each time Jeanne put their plates before them she beamed hugely, touching Adam's shoulders or his hair, and topping up Petra's glass with a rough red wine. Petra noticed that Adam drank only one glass.

'That peach still tasted of the day's sunshine,' Petra said at last. 'You were right: even if I wanted to grumble, I couldn't.'

The intimacy that had budded several hours ago seemed to flower in the dark little room as they sat smiling at each other.

Then, as coffee was put before them in thick green cups, and Adam lit a cigar, he said, 'Where did you learn to play the piano so well?'

'I started when I was young,' Petra answered. 'Then, later, I had some voice training at a place in London.' As his eyebrows rose interestedly, she explained, 'Some girls want to go on the stage; I wanted to be a singer. The piano-playing helped.'

'And what happened to the singing?' His eyes were warm, inviting confidences she had never thought to share with him.

Petra smiled ruefully. 'I simply wasn't good enough. It didn't take too long to realise that I'd never sing Mimi at La Scala.'

For a while they talked about music. Adam's tastes were more wide-ranging than Petra's, and he spoke with a knowledge which revealed his understanding and love of the art. Then he brought the conversation back again to herself.

'So after you gave up your music, what then?'

'Nursing,' Petra told him. 'So instead of Mimi and *Madame Butterfly* I sang Christmas carols with the hospital choir. Sick patients weren't so critical,' she laughed.

'But you gave that up, too.'

'Well,' she said thoughtfully, 'I suppose I got too—involved. A good nurse knows how to keep her emotions under control.'

'And *you* didn't?' There was a note of surprise in his voice.

'Well, let's say that I didn't *then*,' she said quickly.

He seemed about to make a remark, but apparently thought better of it.

Petra finished her coffee, then touched his arm shyly with one fingertip. 'Thank you,' she said softly. 'For this and for the whole day.'

For a moment his hand curved, moving slightly as if it was going to cover her own. She waited, her heart beginning to race, knowing that if at this moment he leaned forward to kiss her across the table he would touch a fount of voluptuousness that had gathered during the hours they had spent together. She wanted him. She knew that now. The realisation was blinding, shattering.

Swiftly she moved her hand. No! something in her mind shrilled. She was not totally ignorant of Adam's ways. He would take what seemed to be offered, exploit it, then think no more of it. But to her it would mean so much more—a giving, a commitment of that part of herself which she could not yet trust while the past was still so close. No more mistakes, she thought desperately. Not ever, if the gods were good. And most certainly not with Adam Herrald!

But almost immediately she realised that her decision was superfluous, for his face had closed against her as if a curtain had dropped between them. As Jeanne reappeared and Adam turned away, Petra noted the tautening of his hard jawline, the cynical, bitter twist of his mouth. They had arrived at this shabby little place in a warm glow of friendship and understanding; for some reason—and perhaps it had something to do with that slight gesture of hers—they were leaving as strangers, almost enemies again.

For the greater part of the journey back they were silent, each mile they travelled seeming to drive them further and further apart. He had withdrawn completely into a hard shell of aloofness. At last Petra felt compelled to break the silence. 'I've thanked you once,' she said with a small laugh, 'but, truly, it's been a lovely day.'

For a moment he didn't answer, and she wished that she hadn't spoken. His silence said more clearly than words that he didn't need her thanks; he had merely fallen in with Venetia's wishes and done his duty. The day was now over, something to be pushed into the background while they both got on with their respective jobs. Then he murmured indifferently, his eyes fixed on the road unwinding before them, 'Well, there's nothing like the wonders of Mother Nature, and a few Roman relics to take one's mind off the chore of looking after three kids.'

Rebuffed, she wanted to protest that that wasn't at all what she had meant, but what was the point? Instead she said briskly, 'You're right. I must tell Venetia what a good idea it all was.'

'Yes, do that.' His voice held a flat note of boredom.

In the darkness Petra's face burned. He certainly knew how to put her in her place! What an idiot she had been, imagining that the day had brought them closer, had established a rapport between them that held more than a touch of magic! And if he, too, had sensed the earlier warmth between them, there was no trace of it in his manner now.

'Well, here we are,' he said blandly, swinging the camper into the drive, the headlights sliding over the toys that the children had left outside, then picking out with startling clarity the dark sheen of a car parked by the front door. 'Guests, it seems,' he murmured. 'Now who the devil can——?'

Light spilled over the gravel as the door opened. For a moment Petra stared, not believing what she saw. Her mouth went dry, then she swallowed, an icy coldness sliding over her.

'Why, it's—it's Marcus,' she whispered.

'Really? And who is Marcus?' But Adam's voice held no curiosity, simply that hateful, frustrating unconcern. And again Petra almost laughed at herself for her earlier fancies. How wrong could one be?

'Marcus is a friend, of course,' she said coldly, getting down from the camper, her heart thumping heavily. What on earth was he doing here? Numbly she walked forward to the figure coming towards her, his hands outstretched, and like a sleepwalker she went on until Marcus's arms closed around her.

Dimly she heard the door of the camper slam behind her as Adam got out, and as Marcus held her possessively she realised that Adam had used the kitchen entrance, presumably tactfully absenting himself from what must appear to be a lovers' reunion.

'But—how did you know where I was?' Petra whispered a few minutes later. She and Marcus sat alone in the big, lamplit room. Apparently Venetia was in the kitchen; perhaps she, too, was being tactful, Petra thought dully.

'Simple,' Marcus said with a laugh. 'I went into the shop.'

'And—and *Di* gave you this address?' Petra stared at him.

He grimaced. 'No, not Di. She's been very cagey over your whereabouts. But she went out, so there was only the other girl—Thea, is it? I saw a postcard lying on the counter and recognised your handwriting. I remarked on it and Thea filled in the details.' There was a smugness in his smile that seemed to applaud his own achievement.

'I see.' Petra's heart seemed to have dropped out of her body. Thea hadn't known just how much she had wished to cover her tracks in case Marcus tried to get in touch with her. But even Petra had never dreamed that he would do more than write to her here. She moistened her lips. 'So you came—all this way . . . But why, Marcus?'

'Isn't it obvious? To see you, of course. Well, no . . . Perhaps it's not *quite* like that . . . Mother decided she wanted to take the waters at some spa or other. I suggested Vals-les-Bains which isn't all that far away from here.' Petra nodded mutely, recalling Mrs Overton's preoccupation with her health, the dyspepsia, the threatening migraines, the imagined ailments, and the miracle cures which rarely outlasted her initial enthusiasm. 'So naturally,' Marcus went on, 'I offered to accompany her.'

'I still don't see why.' Petra shook her head, dazed. 'What was the point of your coming to the villa? And did you—I mean, did you—just show up on the spur of the moment?' What must Venetia have thought? she wondered. She bit her lip, feeling partly responsible for Marcus's intrusion.

'My dear Petra, my manners are better than that, I hope.' He crossed one leg over the other, swinging a highly polished brown shoe. 'No, I telephoned first, of course. This morning, actually, and Mrs Herrald—charming woman—told me that you had gone out but would probably be back in the late afternoon.'

'And you've been waiting here for me since then?'

'Obviously. We didn't expect you to be so late,' he went on, with gentle rebuke. He came over to her and sat on the arm of her chair, taking her hand loosely, then holding a finger significantly. 'When are you going to let me put my ring back? Come on, darling, you've made your point. All right, we quarrelled. We both said things we didn't mean, but——'

'But I *did* mean——'

'Let me finish,' he said indulgently. 'In the heat of the moment we all say things we regret, but we shouldn't be too proud to admit it. I figured that by now you would have come to your senses. Sometimes getting right away is the best thing possible. It helps to get things into perspective. So come on, Petra, let's be sensible and adult about this. Give up this crazy idea and come back to Vals with me. You belong with me, not in some ridiculously menial job. And Mother will be delighted to see you again.'

Petra smothered a hysterical desire to laugh. 'I doubt it,' she said.

Marcus frowned, his mouth tightening. 'I wish you weren't so opposed to her. I can't think why you should be. But you've never liked her, have you?'

Petra closed her eyes wearily. 'Marcus, I refuse to go into all that again. As you've said, we quarrelled. But what I said wasn't merely in the heat of the moment. And I certainly wasn't simply trying to make a point when I gave you back your ring.' She jumped up suddenly and went towards the window, then spun round. 'Oh, what's the use? I've told you all this before . . . So why won't you——? Can't you understand that the very fact of my having to beg you to understand my feelings only demonstrates how out of tune we really are?'

'Rubbish.' He leaned back, his eyes half closed. 'You were happy enough with me once. And I want you for my wife. I just wish you'd stop being so blindly obstinate. And anyway,' he went on smoothly, 'haven't you rather burned your boats? You sold out your share in the business, so what do you propose doing next?'

She lifted her hands vaguely, and noticed with surprise that they shook a little. 'I don't know. I haven't decided . . . Perhaps I'll go to New Zealand. But my future isn't your concern, Marcus. It's pointless of you to keep hounding me like this. So futile . . . It doesn't make the slightest difference to—to us.'

He gave a long-suffering sigh. 'It *could*,' he clipped

out, 'if only you'll be sensible and drop this stubbornness.'

She stared at him, wondering how she could ever have imagined herself in love with him. 'I'm sorry,' she whispered jerkily, 'it's no good, Marcus. Now I'm going to make some tea.' She got out of the room before he could say any more.

In the kitchen Adam was standing by the big table, nursing a large whisky. When Petra came in his eyes flicked over her like cold steel and then, as if the sight of her was more than he could stand, he glanced pointedly away. Venetia was setting out her early-morning tea-tray. She turned to Petra, her eyes lively and enquiring. But before she could speak Adam drawled, 'How exciting for you, Petra! It must seem like Christmas; a *lovely* day out—to use your own words—and then to return and find your boyfriend waiting for you!'

'Yes, isn't it?' Venetia enthused before Petra could answer. 'Your Marcus has been keeping me company ever since I shunted the children off to bed.'

Petra looked from one to the other. He's *not* 'my' Marcus, she wanted to scream. You're both wrong! She felt the hot prick of tears against her eyelids, tears of frustration and disappointment that the day should end like this. Blinking hard, she filled the kettle. 'I'm so sorry, Venetia,' she said at last. 'If I had realised that Marcus intended coming over today, then obviously I wouldn't have gone off with Adam.'

'No, I'm quite sure you wouldn't,' Adam agreed suavely. 'Actually, I thought at the time Venetia suggested the outing that you were rather reluctant. Now I know why.'

'But——' Petra swung round with the truth ready on her lips, but the chill of Adam's expression made her bite it back. Why should she have to explain to *him?* And what difference could it make? She had come close to making a fool of herself with him today, and his earlier attitude still stung. Let him think what he liked! 'As a matter of fact,' she resumed, 'I had no idea that Marcus was in France.' She turned back to Venetia. 'I'm so sorry I wasn't here, and I do hope that——'

'We had a most interesting chat,' Venetia said. 'He told me all about Cranbrook Place. It sounds very grand. I gathered that he wasn't altogether in favour of you taking this job.'

For a moment Petra stared at her. Then her anger at Marcus and the web he had woven mounted. His proprietorial attitude towards her had obviously convinced Venetia that their relationship was serious. He must have painted a picture that greatly exaggerated his own importance in her life. And Venetia, naturally, had accepted it as the true situation. So, too, had Adam. There was a black glint of humour in his eyes as he lounged carelessly against the table, watching her discomfiture, a twist of mockery on his lips. Damn him, she thought miserably. Then she squared her shoulders. Let him assume what he wanted; it made no difference. And, for the time being, it might be easier to go along with the impression that Marcus had created than to embark on the long, involved story which *was* the truth. With Adam watching her like a cat prepared to pounce, she would probably muff her lines anyway.

' . . . and I really don't know where we're going to put him,' Venetia was saying worriedly. 'We can't let him drive back to Vals at this time of night, and obviously you wouldn't want that, Petra. But he won't get into a hotel now, and I can hardly ask him to bed down on the sofa, but——'

'Don't fuss, Venetia,' Adam said laconically. 'I'll sleep in the camper. He can have my bed. No problem.'

'Oh, but really . . .' Petra stared at him stonily. 'I can't ask you to——'

'You're not asking. I'm offering. We must make your boyfriend comfortable while he's here. So stop complicating things, Petra. That's settled, then.'

Again the truth almost spilled out, and again Petra suppressed it. From the very beginning Adam seemed to have had some strange ideas about her; well, let him keep them, whatever they were. The true position or the false one—what difference did it make, for heaven's sake, when their relationship had reverted to the earlier mistrust and enmity? She was too exhausted emotionally to care tonight.

'Then I'll change the sheets.' Venetia got up, but Petra put out a hand.

'No, you've done enough today. I'll see to it.'

'Bless you. I must confess, those children can be exhausting at times,' Venetia smiled. 'You'll find sheets in the linen press on the landing. But have your tea first, and I'll join you if I may. Adam? Are you coming?'

Quickly Petra glanced at Adam. Mockery was still there, making a saturnine mask of his face. He returned her gaze with a knife-edge of contempt in his eyes as he said smoothly, 'Of course I am. Come along, Petra. Hasn't he waited for you long enough today?' He picked up the tray and stood aside in silent taunt until she turned helplessly and followed Venetia out.

Talk was general, but to Petra the air seemed

turbulent with undercurrents. Adam was politely non-committal in his manner, as if dissociating himself from the gathering. Marcus was rather bluff and, Petra thought, talked rather too much about himself. One or twice she caught him glancing at Adam, as if mentally sizing him up. She drank her tea quickly, then escaped upstairs.

She slumped down on Adam's bed. The room seemed to exude the same faint fragrance as his body, almost as if he were here with her. A tie was slung negligently over his dressing mirror; an open book lay on the bedside table, a little heap of loose change on the chest. An unassuageable longing moved within her, mingling with cold sickness at the falsity of the position in which Marcus had placed her. She sat hugging the folded, lavender-scented sheets to herself, rocking gently, as if movement might free her from the tormented treadmill of her thoughts.

For Marcus's visit was doubly unwelcome: it had confirmed something which she hadn't wanted to face. It was as if, confronted with her old feelings for Marcus, she was forced to recognise what she now felt for Adam. In the early days she had never been blind to his attractions, but was able to tell herself that it was an impersonal assessment. After all, she had reasoned, you can admire something without actually wanting it. But now . . .? The longing she had felt in Jeanne's little restaurant returned to swamp her, but in its depths was something more profound than mere physical need.

Torn by sudden violent anger against Marcus, and at herself for falling into the trap of Adam's charisma, she ripped off the pillowcase and sheets and flung them into a heap in the corner. She made up the bed with fierce precision, tucking in the covers tightly, forming neat, mitred corners which would have delighted the heart of any ward sister. There was some relief in speed and action, a temporary escape from the torment of her mind.

She was about to leave the room when she noticed Adam's brushes on the dressing chest, ivory-backed with a silver initial that wasn't his. His father's, she realised, surprised, for she had never thought that Adam had much time for sentiment. She picked up the clothes brush, letting her fingers stroke the smooth, warm ivory, then she spun round guiltily as he came in.

'I need to get a few things,' he said. 'Like, for example, that brush you're holding.'

'I—I was just going to get them together for you,' she whispered. In the light of her recent self-revelation she found it impossible to look at him for a moment. Then she met his eyes in the mirror, and automatically her hands moved, assembling his wallet and blue leather diary as she bent her head, wondering if, in that brief moment, her eyes had betrayed her preposterous, incomprehensible secret.

Adam's hand closed over hers, scalding her. 'Come here. Petra,' he murmured. 'We didn't quite finish our day. There's nothing like bringing things to a logical, satisfactory conclusion, is there? Tying up the loose ends?' His question seemed loaded, but before she could answer she was in his arms, and she had neither the strength nor the will to pull away.

He looked down into her face for a long moment, as if searching for something, then his lips found hers with a swift certainty that took her breath away. His mouth was warm, demanding, lingering upon her own with an intoxication that was almost unbearable. His hands against her spine drew her more closely against him with a firm yet gentle pressure. Every nerve in her body thrilled and clamoured. Her hands went up to his neck, her fingers fluttering against the smooth, warm skin. His lips parted a little against hers, drawing forth a sensuality that rippled over her like hot silk. The tempo of their breathing quickened raggedly, as she gave herself up to a dawning sense of fulfilment. Then his mouth moved away slowly, as if reluctant to lose her kiss, and she felt its caress, feather-light, against the arch of her throat. Her back curved voluptuously, of its own volition, and where his lips touched little frissons of pure pleasure seemed to shimmer under her skin.

The past was forgotten now, all of it—the bitterness, the fury, the confusion that Marcus's visit had created. There was only the present: she and Adam in the room that held the very breath of him.

Within his arms she felt malleable, willing only to be as he wanted her, to follow where he led, knowing that the journey would be an extension of the wonder that sang inside her. She sighed, cupping his face with her hands, drawing up his head that she might look at him.

But what she saw doused her ecstasy more effectively than a cold shower. How, she asked herself blindly, could a man kiss with such tender passion, yet look like this? His eyes, half closed, smouldered, his lips began to curve in a smile of sheer triumph. 'A fitting conclusion,' he breathed. 'I feel like applauding. What a great little actress you are, Petra! You almost convinced me.'

She stared at him, her eyes enormous with pain, trying to understand. 'What . . .? Adam, I . . . What do you mean?' she whispered. She seemed to be in the grip of a nightmare. 'I—can't imagine—what——'

'Can't you?' he said softly. 'Can't you really?' His smile sent ice-water through her veins. Then he shrugged. 'Well, does it really matter? And explanations can be tedious, so why bother?' His voice hardened suddenly. 'Hadn't you better go down? Your boyfriend awaits you.'

Those kisses might never have happened, she thought, aghast. Adam was as composed and unmoved as she had ever seen him.

She opened her mouth to protest, but Adam went on inexorably, 'After all, he's come panting all the way from Casterleigh just to see you. Absence makes the heart grow fonder, they say. Was that part of the reason you took this job? Well, it seems to have worked, doesn't it? He's already waited here for hours. Such devotion!' The contempt in his tone matched the curl of his lips.

As if on cue, Marcus's voice floated up, 'Petra, darling, it's taking you a long time——'

Wordlessly, still disbelieving, Petra stared up at Adam, her head shaking slightly from side to side. Then she stumbled from the room, Adam's low, mocking laughter reverberating through her head.

She slept badly, waking unrefreshed early the next morning. As she went down to the kitchen to make tea, she passed the open door of the sitting-room and saw, to her surprise, that Marcus was already up. He had opened the french windows overlooking the pool and was sitting just inside the room, staring out. In the bright morning he looked incongruously formal in his grey suit and collar and tie.

Petra's heart sank as she pushed back her hair and tightened the belt of her housecoat. 'You're up early,' she said numbly. 'I'm making tea. Like a cup?'

He stood up politely. He seemed very earnest, and Petra's heart dropped further, guessing that he would use these private moments to pursue the old argument. What did it take to get through to him? she wondered dully. She couldn't stand much more.

When she was sitting opposite him he surprised her by saying suddenly, 'Is there anything between you and Herrald?'

'Of course not,' she breathed, flushing. 'Why should you ask that?'

'It just crossed my mind, that's all.' He frowned. 'You are telling me the truth, Petra?'

Coming so soon after Adam's judgement the previous evening, she felt a flare of anger. Why should she have to prove her honesty—to either of these two men, for heaven's sake? 'I am telling you the truth,' she said from between clenched teeth.

'All right; no need to get angry. I accept it. So that's not the reason why you won't come back with me to Vals?'

Exasperated, she closed her eyes and resisted the urge to bang her cup down and walk out. 'Marcus,' she said with slow intensity, 'I refuse to go into all that yet again. For heaven's sake, can't you get it into your head that——'

'You loved me once,' he said accusingly.

'I thought I did,' she corrected in a gentler tone. 'And then I realised—and don't ask me how—that I didn't love you *enough*. Oh, Marcus, I could never have become the kind of wife you want. I'm sorry. So sorry . . .' She went over to him and knelt by his chair, taking one of his hands between hers, and looking up at him compassionately. 'Look, what possible chance of success would a marriage have if—if the bride feels this way *before* the wedding? It would be doomed from the start. And can't you see, I would be doing you a great wrong if I married you, feeling this way? And it would be a sin against myself, too—against my own—integrity.' She stopped suddenly; how Adam would have laughed at that! Then she made herself go on. 'I know that you would prefer to think that all this is the result of a mere lovers' quarrel. But, believe me, it's much more than that. And surely by now my words and my—actions have convinced you.'

Marcus stared at her, his face suddenly pinched and small. 'I'd hoped to take you back with me,' he said doggedly. 'We could have celebrated our re-engagement with a special dinner tonight. But you're stubborn, Petra. For heaven's sake, what more can I do to——'

'Nothing,' she said wildly. 'There *is* nothing more for us. Don't tell me you're thinking that, given a little more time, a little more persuasion, you can break me in like—like one of your horses, and lead me back on the end of a bridle?' Her voice broke a little. 'You can't do that with people.'

'Of course I didn't think anything of the sort,' he snapped.

'Look,' she entreated, pressing his hand in her intensity, 'I don't love you enough. I'm sorry, but I can't force my feelings. It's as simple as that. Why not face up to it? And you know,' she went on gently, 'I was never as important to you as a woman should be to the man who professes to love her. I can see that clearly. You must, too. It was obvious in many tiny ways, but at the time I . . .' She shrugged. 'If you'll only give yourself a chance to reflect, and stop trying to hold on to something that——'

She heard a noise and glanced through the open french windows. Adam was cleaving a swift, smooth path through the aquamarine water of the pool. He must have seen them, Petra realised, sitting close like lovers, holding hands. Her face grew hot; she dropped Marcus's hand and stood up.

After a moment he got up, too. 'Well,' he said stiffly, 'you certainly seem to know what you *don't* want. You might regret this, you know. But you can't say I didn't try to patch things up. However . . . I'd better go. Perhaps you would thank Mrs Herrald for her hospitality, and tell her I was anxious to get back. Obviously it's been a wasted journey for me.'

Heavy-eyed, Petra watched the hired car drive away. Already, before the day had properly begun, she felt exhausted. Burying her face in her hands, she wondered if she would ever again be able to think straight. She seemed to have run the gamut of all human emotion in the past twenty-four hours—happiness, bewilderment, pain, anger, incomprehension, deception . . . How life could change, from one minute to the next!

She went back upstairs and showered briskly, trying to pull herself together and expunge from her mind everything that had happened since she had climbed up into the camper only the previous morning.

If there was one tiny grain of comfort to be gained, it was the conviction that at least Marcus wouldn't be bothering her again.

She busied herself putting out clean clothes for the children, and when they all went down to breakfast she saw that the camper had already left. Adam had decided to make an early start, Venetia told her. And Petra was thankful for that, and the fact that it was Monique's day off and therefore a busy day for herself.

* * *

'You know, Marcus isn't really my boyfriend,' Petra said suddenly as she and Venetia prepared supper in the kitchen. For some reason it seemed important that Venetia, at least, was not deceived by Marcus's appearance. 'We were engaged once, but——' She shrugged. 'It didn't work out so far as I was concerned.'

'I see,' Venetia said carefully. 'I thought you looked—troubled,' she mused. 'What strange creatures we humans are; never so happy as when we're in love, and yet the pain it causes! The misunderstandings, the vulnerability . . .' She smiled wryly. 'Wouldn't you think we would have the sense to avoid it, learn from our mistakes?'

'Well, I think I have.' Petra forced a bright note.

Venetia grimaced, deftly washing lettuce. 'Oh, I doubt if we ever really learn. After one bad experience we tell ourselves that we're saner or wiser, and then subconsciously we give ourselves a different reason for doing the same thing all over again with someone else. Isn't that how it goes?'

'I suppose so. Marcus will soon find someone else.'

'Poor Marcus. Well, let's hope he does. Hope springs eternal . . . and all that.' Venetia smiled. 'The marvellous thing is that, in the end, it often works out wonderfully. I suppose that's why we go on subconsciously searching.' She gave Petra's hand a motherly pat. 'It must have been embarrassing for you, my dear . . . I mean, Marcus turning up here as if he had every right to. Well, put it behind you now. One day things will come right for you and for him. Just as they did for me and my Richard, and for Adam and Merrill.'

Merrill! The name cracked like a pistol shot in Petra's memory. Adam's wife. But surely Venetia was wrong there?

She moistened suddenly dry lips and said tentatively, 'So Adam and his wife were—were happily married?' Just saying the words seemed to grind something in her heart.

'Very happy, I would say, in spite of big differences in their personalities.' Venetia continued dribbling oil into the mayonnaise thoughtfully. 'Confidentially, I didn't take too readily to Merrill. But of course,' she went on firmly, 'I didn't see much of her. In fact, I hardly knew her. She was rather—reserved. But together they seemed . . . right.'

'But . . . But then, why did they divorce?' The question seemed ripped from Petra's lips. 'Oh, I'm sorry,' she hurried on, 'it's none of my——'

'Divorce?' Venetia stared. 'Who on earth told you that?'

Petra shook her head helplessly, trying to think back. Then after a moment she said quietly, 'No one. I knew that Adam had been married, but was no longer . . . And I suppose I simply assumed . . .'

'Merrill died.' For a moment Venetia concentrated on her mixing, and Petra found herself sinking down on to a stool, the strength ebbing from her body. 'Adam was driving her to the airport,' Venetia resumed softly. 'Merrill had an assignment in—Rome, I think it was. They were late. There was a patch of oil on the road . . . The car skidded and hit a tree. Adam walked away, but——'

'How dreadful,' Petra breathed. She felt stunned. She stared up at Venetia, her eyes like soft golden flames, her hands slack in her lap. 'And how tragic for him.' The shock of Venetia's story had driven all other thoughts out of her mind. She could only guess at the depths of Adam's suffering; memory gave her a brief flashback to the first moments of meeting him. She had read pain in his face then, and the stoicism of bearing it. So this was the reason!

Unseeing, she resumed slicing tomatoes. Perhaps it gave a clue to Adam's baffling behaviour in the early days: his first resentment of her, his later attempts at dalliance. It didn't explain everything, of course, but he wouldn't be the first man to take consolation wherever he could find it.

'Yes.' Venetia sighed. 'Fortunately Merrill died instantly, so it could have been worse. That is what I told myself and tried to tell Adam. But he seemed to switch off. He would never talk about it. It must have been a devastating blow for him because, naturally, he would feel that he was to blame. And guilt, whether it's real or assumed, is a terrible thing to live with. It must be hell for him.'

Petra nodded miserably. All this must have some part in the bitter complexities of the man. And it might even be that the children's obvious liking for herself had reminded him of their affection for Merrill. She remembered that anguished, haunted kiss in Moulins. Had he wanted to punish her for usurping a sacred memory? She frowned suddenly, her knife still. No, there was something wrong with *that* theory, for hadn't Sarah confided that she had no affection for Adam's wife?

Petra got up and went to rinse her hands. She had certainly made a big mistake in assuming that Adam's marriage had ended because he was impossible to live with. Apparently she couldn't have been more wrong!

A wound seemed to have opened up inside her, yet she couldn't resist probing it.

'Was Merrill a photographer, too?' she asked after a moment.

'No, she was a model. A very attractive girl, but there were times when she seemed almost unreal. As a matter of fact, sometimes when I look at——' Venetia stopped, her head cocked. 'I think I hear him now. Let's change the subject. He would hate to know that we've been talking about him.'

A moment later the camper door slammed in the drive, followed by the sound of another car door closing and muted voices and laughter which grew louder. Then the kitchen door opened.

Petra bent over the basil she was chopping for the tomato salad. She couldn't bring herself to look at Adam. She hated him for deliberately and cold-bloodedly arousing her with his kisses last night, then demolishing her emotions with calculated cruelty. And yet, even so, something in her reached out to him.

Then she heard him say, 'One guest leaves, another arrives. I found her wandering around Ruoms, looking for us.'

Venetia went forward, and at last Petra was forced to look up. Caroline Benton stood in the doorway, a frankly appealing smile on her face.

'Venetia, this is Caroline,' Adam said smoothly. 'We've known each other for some time. She'll be staying for a little while, if that's all right?'

'Well, of course it is, you know that,' Venetia exclaimed. 'Come along, my dear. You don't know Petra——'

'Oh, Petra and I are old friends,' Caroline murmured, to Petra's amazement.

'Hello, Caroline,' she murmured, returning Caroline's smile. She still found herself unable to look in Adam's direction, although every nerve in her was pricklingly aware of him standing there. She turned to

Venetia. 'Adam's room?' she asked brightly. And, when Venetia nodded, said, 'I'll go and get it ready, then.'

She went out, thankful to escape.

CHAPTER SEVEN

'TO GIVE Caroline her due,' Venetia said amiably, three days later, 'she's easy to get along with. And as Adam takes her off with him during the day, we hardly notice she's here.'

Petra and Venetia were in the kitchen putting the finishing touches to the evening meal. Outside the children were playing an argumentative game of *boules.* 'And,' Venetia went on, mixing fresh fruit salad deftly, 'she eats almost nothing. I'm not surprised she's so thin.'

Petra smiled. 'She's a model, so I expect that's the idea,' she said, determinedly shutting her mind to any speculation about Caroline and Adam.

Caroline had slipped easily into place at the villa, and Adam seemed happy in her company. Petra bit her lip. Against her will, memories of the day she had spent with Adam crept back at times, and she would try to block him out of her mind. Obviously, he must find Caroline attractive—what man wouldn't? And it had certainly taken the heat off herself. Although, she concluded dismally, the heat was already off; Adam hadn't minced his words that evening in his room. And then, the following morning, he had witnessed her last scene with Marcus and would have drawn the obvious conclusions.

She sighed, realising that now, at last, she was getting just what she had intended out of this job—a total absorption in the welfare and happiness of the children, with no distractions at all from Adam.

Over dinner that evening Adam spoke about his day's work. His conversation with Venetia, occasionally interrupted by a remark from Caroline, drifted over Petra's head as she concentrated on getting Thomas to eat, but when Adam spoke her name she could not avoid looking at him. '. . . some superb flower close-ups,' he said. 'They'll interest you, Petra.' Unreadable eyes were fixed upon her above a polite smile. Dinner-table chat, she thought. Nothing more than that. And yet she was sensitive to something below the surface. It was as if he had noticed that she was avoiding any sort of contact with him and was determined to impose his presence upon her. 'Green hellebore, to name but one. Butterflies, too, and hawks circling——'

'And a snake,' Caroline said, with a shudder.

'I wish *I* could come with you,' Sarah put in. '*I* like flowers and butterflies, too,' she added plaintively.

Caroline rarely spoke directly to the children, but now she smiled. 'You'd probably find it boring,' she murmured patronisingly.

'I wouldn't, though. I *like* being with Adam,' Sarah argued stubbornly. 'If you weren't here,' she went on, ignoring her grandmother's warning glance, 'he'd probably take me with him sometimes.'

'Then why not come along with Caroline and me tomorrow?' Adam suggested.

Petra was holding out a dish of chicken to Caroline, and saw the red-tipped hand pause momentarily. Then Caroline said smoothly, 'Yes, why don't you? I won't be going, though.' She looked appealingly in Venetia's direction. 'Is that all right? I mean, if I just laze around here? I've been bitten by your flying things today, devoured alive, in fact.'

'I've got some lotion for that,' Venetia said. 'And of

course it's all right, my dear. Driving around the countryside in this weather can't be anyone's idea of fun.'

It certainly wouldn't be Caroline's, Petra agreed silently. But perhaps it was when the driving stopped that Caroline's fun began. She wondered if Adam was disappointed by Caroline's decision, but his face revealed nothing.

'And we're off to a party tonight,' Caroline said, 'so it'll be a relief not to have to get up early in the morning.' But she softened her words with a lingering smile in Adam's direction.

In the early hours of the morning Petra lay in bed wondering what had wakened her. Then she heard footsteps on the gravel below, the murmur of voices; Adam and Caroline returning from the party, she thought dully.

Petra had sensed earlier that Caroline was the kind of woman who would happily sink her claws into any man she fancied, although those claws would be sheathed in velvet.

But Adam? How did he feel about it? Petra wondered. She closed her eyes, wishing that questions and answers would stop revolving like a treadmill in her mind. Who knew what Adam felt about anything? Still, he seemed happy enough to have Caroline here at the villa.

Petra's mind flipped back yet again to the day she had spent with him. The day when everything had gone right. A day to remember, always, and not just for the sights he had shown her. It had had a—a burnish, a perfection. A bright awareness of life and living that placed it far above other pleasant days. She closed her eyes, squeezing back the tears, and thumped her pillow impatiently. Why were such thoughts more potent at night?

Restlessly, she turned on her side and groped for the water jug on the table. Empty. She sighed. She would give Adam and Caroline a little time to get to their respective beds, then she'd go down and refill it.

Over in the other bed Sarah stirred, and Petra lay still until she heard the door of Adam's room—now Caroline's—close. Then she shrugged into her housecoat and went down.

She was opening the fridge door when a voice behind her whispered, 'Midnight feasts?'

She jumped. 'Oh, it's you,' she said crossly, her heart beginning to knock.

'Disappointed? Who were you expecting?' His voice was lazy, his words faintly slurred.

'Don't be ridiculous,' she snapped. 'I was thirsty, that's all . . .'

'And sleepless, too. We can't have that, can we? It might impair your efficiency.' Amusement threaded his tone as he watched her speculatively.

Seeing him alone so unexpectedly after the strain of the last days stretched her self-control almost to breaking-point. He looked infuriatingly urbane standing there in the blue and white kitchen. His white jacket hung casually but elegantly from one shoulder, as if he was confident that whatever he wore, and however he wore it, he would inevitably look right. A secret humour danced in his eyes above the heart-tilting, crooked smile, and Petra felt as if she had walked into the wrong house, a building rife with disturbance. She didn't understand him, and probably never would. But she loved him. And the only thing that mattered was getting out, back to the safety of her room, beyond his reach.

She depressed the lever on the little reservoir inside

the fridge door and stared hard at the cold water streaming into the glass jug. 'Don't let me keep you,' she said smoothly. 'And don't worry about the lights. I'll turn them off when you've gone. Goodnight, Adam.'

'Do you know,' he drawled, 'I do believe I'll join you.' He drew out two chairs from the big table. 'We might as well make ourselves comfortable.'

'I'm on my way back to bed,' she reminded him sharply.

'Oh, must you? It seems so long since we had a chat. And don't you find this rather romantic—you and I awake on a summer night, alone in a sleeping house? Anyway, I loathe drinking alone.' He got up and poured himself a whisky.

He was like a predator, she thought, stalking its prey, goading it into doing something foolish, then he would move in for the kill. Her instinct for self-preservation told her to go. But it would boost his ego immensely to know that she needed to hide from him, and she had no intention of offering herself up as a sacrifice to his ego.

'All right,' she murmured offhandedly, pulling her chair a little further from his and sitting down. 'Was it a good party?' she said at last, when the silence had built up to an uncomfortable pressure.

'Very,' he said politely, but the gleam in his eyes mocked her attempts to treat this encounter as a necessary bore. 'I've known Rob and Mary Michael for some time. Francophiles like myself, but they got out of the rat-race at home and came here.'

'And Caroline?' It was masochism, but Petra couldn't stop herself. 'Did she enjoy it, too?'

'Of course. Caroline's a party girl. Or hadn't you noticed?' He gave Petra a sidelong glance.

Yes, Petra thought bitterly, I had noticed. Caroline had departed wearing a simple black dress that had probably cost the earth. She had looked almost inhumanly *soignée.* No doubt she came into her own at a glittering gathering, and Adam would have been the envy of the other men there. She took a steadying sip of water.

'Incidentally,' he was saying, 'they—Rob and Mary, that is—are holding a fancy-dress party on Saturday. We're invited.'

'How nice for you,' Petra said stiltedly. She wondered just how much longer she could go on sitting there, making futile conversation.

'And for you, too. You're invited.' The smile flickered cruelly.

'How can I be? I don't even know these people.'

'That doesn't matter,' he drawled. 'I've fixed it. I'm taking you and Caroline. I do hope that you two girls hit it off together.'

He knows the answer to that one, Petra thought. So why *had* he fixed it? To make Caroline jealous, perhaps? Was that part of his game? She stood up suddenly and gave him a bright, distant smile. 'Thanks for fixing the party for me, but I don't think I'll go. However, it was—considerate of you to think of me.'

He made a deprecating movement of his shoulders under the loose drape of white jacket. 'Oh, I can be very thoughtful at times, Petra. Especially if it's in a deserving cause.'

She spun round. 'How philanthropic,' she murmured. 'Comfort to the needy? A night out for the hired help? Like that day you so graciously gave up for me?'

'Don't be so bloody proud!' He was on his feet suddenly, looming over her. His easy, languid manner had hardened grittily. The lazy half-smile was gone. His hands were on her shoulders, his fingers biting into her flimsily covered flesh. He gave her a little shake. 'What the hell's the matter with you, Petra?' For a moment his eyes burned into hers with a flare of intense black fire.

She moved suddenly, shrugging off his hands. 'I don't know what you're suggesting,' she said breathlessly. 'It's late, and I'm tired. Proud? What's that got to do with anything? I think you've had too much to drink and——'

'Not when I'm driving,' he barked. 'Never then, and *I* should——' He bit off his words suddenly as she faked a luxurious yawn.

'So tired,' she murmured, picking up the jug. 'You'll see to the lights, then?'

He gave an exclamation of baffled fury which she ignored.

She went slowly upstairs. Her legs felt weak, but her heart was banging thunderously. The short conversation had drained her. No, she amended, not the conversation. Just him. And the intimacy of the setting, and her own instinctive response to his male magnetism. How easily he could demolish her!

So, if he expected her to go to that fancy-dress party, he could think again!

'Oh, but you *should* go,' Venetia insisted on Saturday afternoon. 'It'll be fun for you, a chance to meet people. I know you love the children, but too much of their company is a bit limiting.' She touched Petra's hand. 'We can soon rustle up a costume for you,' she went on quickly, as Petra started to speak. 'There's a trunkful of stuff upstairs. Sarah used to dress up when she was smaller, and I'm a real squirrel about hoarding things. So we'll put our heads together and think of something stunning. You need have no worries on that score.'

Petra took a small, desperate sip of tea. 'But my place is here,' she protested weakly, 'with the children. After all, I *am* being paid for it.' She fixed her gaze on an orange-and lemon-coloured butterfly. 'That reminds me,' she went on, hurriedly changing the subject, 'we need lemons for that sorbet, so if you like I'll go——'

'It's high time you had a night out.' Venetia's tone was decisive. Then she turned, frank grey eyes fixed on Petra's face enquiringly. 'Or is there some particular reason why you don't want to go? Something to do with—Adam?'

Petra glanced away. 'Of course not,' she said emphatically. 'Why should there be? Anyway, he'll be with Caroline——'

'Yes.' The grey eyes were clouded now, the smooth brow drawn into a puzzled frown. Suddenly Petra could read Venetia's mind: despite her apparent tolerance, she didn't really like Caroline. Could it be that she was concerned about Caroline becoming the—second Mrs Adam Herrald? Was that what Venetia was uneasy about? Caroline—prospective daughter-in-law?

Petra stared over the garden with its mauve festoons of wistaria, the foaming oleander, and across to the little peach orchard where Edouard had set up the sprinkler. One day Caroline could be mistress of this lovely place; Caroline, with her sharp, dramatic beauty, her sophistication, her indifference to children . . . Was that what Venetia saw?

She looked again at the older woman and smothered a sigh of resignation. 'All right, you've talked me into it. In which case, I'd better start getting a costume together.'

'Damn,' Petra muttered as she went upstairs. Why am I doing this? she thought. I've been out-manouevred by Venetia. And it's none of my business. Why can't the Herralds sort out their own affairs? Why must I be embroiled? If Adam's in love with Caroline, then it's his affair. He's old enough, for heaven's sake, and nothing that Venetia or I can do will change that.

She could hear the whirr of the sewing machine from the little room at the end of the landing. Caroline had laid first claim to it after returning from town with several parcels.

The trunk yielded nothing that fired Petra's imagination, and after a few minutes she went back to her bedroom. For a long time she stared at the silvery-grey tunic in her wardrobe. It had belonged to her grandmother, and Petra had found it among her mother's things. A simple, high-necked top, encrusted with broad, frosty stripes of clear glass beads down the sleeves, across the yoke and down the front.

She had put it into her luggage as an afterthought when she had packed for this job, not knowing then quite what to expect at the villa. With a simple black skirt it made a suitable outfit for a formal dinner. But with a pair of daring tight silver trousers, Di had pronounced it 'sensational'.

Petra's thoughts ran on . . . With her pale hair dressed in spikes, and some diamanté stones from that tangle of trimmings in the trunk . . . She could stick them on to the backs of her hands, one or two along her cheekbones . . . She went down to the kitchen for the scissors.

* * *

'And what are *you* supposed to be?' Adam said later. His eyes moved over her with a glint in their depths that she had come to mistrust. It spoke of amusement. Or was it derision? Either way, it whipped her tautly strung nerves as they waited in the hall for Caroline to come down.

Petra tilted up her face, returning Adam's stare with a cool hazel glance that hid her wretchedness. The tiny, brilliant stones on her cheekbones caught the light and glittered frostily. 'An icicle,' she said shortly. She seemed to see the vista of the whole miserable evening stretched ahead. Already she was wishing she had resisted Venetia's persuasion.

'Of course,' he said heartily. 'How stupid of me.'

'Yes, wasn't it? And what exactly are *you* supposed to be?' She tried to look at him impersonally, but the flowing black cape he wore gave an added drama to his looks. The tight, short jacket revealed the long, masculine line of hip and thigh. The wide black sombrero that hung on his shoulders suited him in some high theatrical way that burned his image into her mind.

'A Spanish grandee. But don't blame me. Venetia got this thing together.'

He turned as, with a silken rustle, Caroline appeared at the top of the stairs where she paused for a moment, then moved down sinuously. Her hair was tightly dressed into a shiny, intricate coil at the back of her head. In its dark sheen a red satin flower gleamed. Her bright, multi-frilled skirt was slit in the centre to give provocative glimpses of her legs as she moved, and the plain black top with its long, tight sleeves emphasised her tiny waist.

As she reached them she raised a graceful hand and flicked open a red lace fan, looking at Adam over its edge. A faint, musky perfume wafted towards Petra like a breath of sin.

'This should be fun,' Caroline murmured. 'Adam, you look devastating.' Her eyes were warm above the red lace as she removed an invisible hair from his cloak, patting his shoulder with a proprietorial gesture. 'Are we ready?' She turned, her smile encompassing Petra. 'You look quite—different.' She raised her eyebrows. 'What, exactly, is it?'

'Isn't it obvious?' Adam put it suavely. 'Petra's an icicle.'

'Oh? How original, in this climate. Yes, I suppose I can see that now.' She lowered her lashes over eyes that had sharpened suddenly. 'Are you intending to melt away?' she said sweetly, with a silvery tinkle of laughter.

'Oh, definitely,' Petra answered. 'Icicles usually do, you know, given time.'

She had no intention of getting in the way of Adam and Caroline, and she just prayed that these people—Rob and Mary Michael—would be hospitable enough to make that easy for her. Privately, she was beginning to regret her idea for the costume. Caroline had made certain that her own dress was essentially feminine and flattering. Lightly Petra touched the stiff, unfamiliar spikes of her short hair and wondered if perhaps she hadn't overdone things. But it was too late to change anything now. She just wanted to get through the evening as best she could, and hoped that she would soon be absorbed into other company, giving Adam and Caroline a wide berth.

To her surprise, however, she discovered later that there was something disarmingly liberating about fancy dress. It was as if, once among the sheikhs and houris, the Pierrots and black cats, she had shed her normal everyday shelf. Tonight she was no longer Petra Macey, she was simply an anonymous icicle. And after three champagne cocktails she realised that she felt quite light-hearted. Her inhibitions were gone and, for once, she felt completely in command. Was this why some people wore dark glasses, she pondered—as a kind of disguise to conceal their real, vulnerable selves from the crowd? She glanced up and caught Adam's quizzical glance upon her.

'Don't you think you've had enough?' he murmured as she reached for a glass from the tray of drinks held out by a circulating waiter.

She turned a brilliant smile upon him. 'Of course not. I'm having *fun*. Don't be a wet blanket, Adam. You should be pleased. Isn't this what you had in mind for me when you so *thoughtfully* included me in the invitation?'

She turned as a hand touched her arm, and moved away with a yellow-turbanned rajah. Automatically Adam reached out and took the glass from her. 'You won't be needing this,' he said tightly.

'Why don't *you* try dancing?' Petra said to him over her shoulder. 'It might relax you a bit.'

The rajah drew her into his arms and they found a small space near the french windows. 'And what are you?' he said, his voice heavily accented. His eyes were green and lively, his teeth very white in his dark beard.

'An icicle,' she grinned.

'Pliz? What is—eye-sickle?'

'Oh, heavens,' she murmured vaguely. 'I should have taken a crash course in French.'

'You say . . .? Pliz?' His arms drew her closely to him as they swayed to the music.

'An icicle—it is . . . *C'est—c'est* . . .' She frowned, trying to concentrate, then glanced up to see the roguish sparkle in his eyes. 'I think,' she said severely, 'that you know perfectly well what an icicle is.'

He laughed. 'Of course I do, darling. But who are you, anyway? Or shall I just call you *darling?*'

'My name's Petra Macey. But call me what you like, so long as it's nice.'

'I think *darling* suits you. And what are you doing here? I know most of Rob and Mary's friends, but I've never met you before.' His hands moved up to lie over her shoulder-blades. 'I would have remembered if I had,' he went on softly.

She laughed. This was how life should be, she thought cloudily. Smiles, pleasantness, compliments—everyone being nice to each other . . . No black, sombre looks. No punishing kisses or baffling accusations. 'But how would you know if we *had* met?' she teased. 'I don't usually go around looking like this, you know.'

'Ah,' he said softly. 'But some things—like eyes the colour of highland burns in sunlight—are not to be forgotten easily. And whatever else you might do to yourself, you can't alter your eyes. So, to repeat myself, what are you doing here?'

'I came with Adam Herrald. I work for the family temporarily. How about you?'

'I'm on a sailing holiday. The boat's tied up in Marseilles. We hired a car and are touring the hinterland for a few days. Naturally one looks up old friends.' His arms tightened. 'Am I going to see you again? After tonight, I mean?' His eyelids drooped suggestively. 'Do say *yes.* How about tomorrow, for instance?'

'Aren't you rushing things a little?' she said playfully.

He grinned in mock-ruefulness. 'That's my downfall. They'll engrave it on my tombstone. "He rushed the ladies." But why not? Time's short, so why mess about?'

'There's such a thing as *finesse,*' she pointed out, smiling.

'Oh, *that.*' He dismissed it with a twirl that made her

head spin. 'That was for yesteryear.'

This conversation was becoming sillier by the minute, Petra thought blithely, but it seemed years since she had felt so carefree. 'Who are you, anyway, when you're not being a rajah?'

'Call me Sam. Sam Sheridan, actually.' She felt the prickle of his beard against her forehead as he held her even closer. 'I never thought an icicle could be so warm and sexy.'

She leaned back, flashing him a sceptical glance from under her lashes. 'Is Sam short for Samson, by any chance?' she quipped.

'Of course,' he grinned. 'Don't you recognise the strong-man tactics?'

'I was only asking,' she murmured. She closed her eyes and the pleasant, slightly elevated sensation grew. She could dance for ever in this way, she felt. Dance and laugh and never make another sensible, serious remark in her life. Never give another thought to Adam . . . Never let him wreak havoc with her emotions——

Then she felt Sam's arms slacken and drop away. For a moment she held on to him. Then she looked up questioningly and turned to follow his gaze.

'I'm cutting in,' Adam said tersely. 'So when you're *quite* ready, Petra——'

'Just my luck,' Sam murmured, 'and I'm crazy for icicles. But I'll be back, darling.' Petra watched him go, a sense of panic rising in her.

'I'm glad to see you're having fun,' Adam said idly, one arm sliding round her waist. 'I told you that you would.'

He moved smoothly, holding her in a firm, close grip so that they seemed to dance as one. Desperately she tried to claw back the light-hearted nonsense that had come so easily in response to Sam's inane chatter. But it had gone now, and she prayed that the music would end quickly.

'So you did,' she said at last. 'And, as always, you were right,' she added sarcastically, willing herself to resist the persuasion of the dreamy music and the whisper of his thighs against her body. Little currents of sensation began to tingle through her, and she stiffened, jerking her head back to search the crowd for Sam, hoping to signal him back.

'Looking for someone?' Adam said pleasantly. Then, as she turned her head again, 'Why did you have to fix your hair in those damn spikes?'

'Part of the image,' she snapped.

'And, for some reason,' he went on thoughtfully, 'you seem to be as prickly as your hair.' He tightened his hold so that, against her will, her head lay against his chest. She could feel his heartbeat under her cheek, strong and rhythmic. The magnetism of his nearness flooded back to dominate her with a force that was frightening. He had too much influence over her, and he probably knew it instinctively, revelling in his power.

'Where's Caroline?' she said lightly. 'I thought she was supposed to be with you.'

'You're *both* with me,' he said conclusively.

'*Are* we?' Glancing up at him her gaze was gripped by the unwavering intensity of his black stare, as if he wanted to see into her mind, her soul. The tremor inside her strengthened and she looked away, feeling her panic quicken into a spasm. Just what did he have that could switch her moods so violently, injecting fire or ice into her blood, confusing her so completely that she could both love and hate him at the same time, while he seemed to remain unmoved?

'So we are,' she said crisply, 'but not in quite the

same way, I think.'

'No,' he murmured, 'I agree there *is* a difference.'

She saw Sam coming towards her and moved away from Adam with relief. 'Why, here's Sam,' she said lightly. 'Short for Samson, I believe. Perhaps he's come to carry me off.' In her own ears her words sounded idiotic.

'If you must know,' Adam said, 'his name is Newsam, not Samson. And don't set your hopes too high, Petra. He doesn't look all that strong to me.'

'Is that supposed to pass for wit?' Petra murmured. 'Because if so——'

'And besides,' Adam pursued inexorably, 'I'm taking you in to supper now. If you're going to take any more of those cocktails you ought to have something to eat——'

'Taking me in to supper?' she breathed in mock-submission. 'Are you really?' She raised her eyebrows and the little brilliant stones at her temples danced, reflecting brittle chips of light. 'You're so decisive, masterful . . . So very macho——' She winced as the grip on her arm tightened, and Sam Sheridan paused before her uncertainly. 'I'm sorry,' she said, hiding her chagrin. 'I'm going to supper with Adam. I'll see you later, Sam.' She lifted her chin. 'Unfortunately, I have to do more or less what he says. He's my employer in a kind of way, and I suppose I'm in no position to refuse.' She was rewarded by Adam's sharp intake of breath, and knew that her words had stung.

'All right, then.' Sam gave a Gallic shrug, spreading his hands. 'But don't forget, we haven't fixed that date yet.' He turned, melting into the bright throng.

'Was that really necessary?' Adam said coldly as they moved to the edge of the crowd. 'The employer part?'

'I like to keep the record straight,' Petra answered

with equal chill. Then, 'My goodness, Caroline looks furious.'

Over by the wall Caroline was talking to a tall, cadaverous man soberly dressed in black dinner-jacket. Her eyes were fixed on Petra in a gaze of blue venom.

'I can't imagine why,' Adam said curtly. 'That's Scott Farrand she's talking to. And he can do her career quite a lot of good.'

'But maybe Caroline isn't too interested in her career at this very moment,' Petra said indifferently.

Adam merely raised an eyebrow as he slid his hand under Petra's elbow and led her out into a conservatory which ran the width of the house. It was grouped with cane chairs and tables among the greenery and flowers.

Petra stared at the long table with its attractively laid buffet, then looked away. 'I'm not at all hungry——' she began. She did indeed feel rather sick. That could be due to the champagne cocktails, but she knew it wasn't. Butterflies seemed to be congregating in her stomach. Apart from two other people sitting at one end of the conservatory and the waiters standing ready behind the table, she and Adam were alone, and she was nervous. 'Anyway, I—I think we're a little early,' she went on uncertainly.

Adam didn't answer. The silence seemed charged with dangerous electricity. Her need for escape increased, but his hand on her arm seemed to pin her to the spot where she stood. Mentally she shook herself, taking a deep, steadying breath and jerking her arm away. 'You stay and eat,' she said. 'I need some air, so——'

'Then I'll come with you.'

'Really,' she snapped, 'I'm quite capable of looking after myself. You're not my keeper. So, thanks for the offer, but——' Her voice rose a little in desperation as he propelled her through the doors and down a short flight of stone steps leading down to the garden. Why couldn't he have stayed with Caroline? Why did he have to muscle in? She could cope with the Sams of this world; they meant nothing. But Adam Herrald was something else.

'But my dear,' he drawled softly, 'I wouldn't dream of leaving you alone. Who knows, your friend—*Samson*—might choose the moment to carry you off. And after that champagne you might—be shall we say—vulnerable? Or is that what you're wanting?' His tone hardened, spitting out the words. 'Is that it? Am I spoiling your fun, Petra? Is *that* what's ruffling your feathers tonight?'

Then, cataclysmically, she was in his arms, crushed against him in a spasm of strength. She stared up. His face was twisted with anger. Moonlight burnished the high cheekbones, the line of the aquiline noise. His eyes were a dark glitter, his face devilish in the intensity of its mockery. Then, with mercurial swiftness, his lips came down to plunder her soft, unbelieving mouth.

Instantly she felt a contradictory, answering thrill. Suddenly exalted, she seemed to rise out of herself on fierce wings. *This,* something in her brain shouted, *this* was all she wanted. The rest, the irritations, the misery, were nothing while there was *this.* The strength of his hands as they explored her back whipped her senses to a clamour. His touch brought a swift annihilation of all logic. There were a million reasons why this should not happen, but the one reason why it should far outweighed them. She felt his sensuality fanning the flame of her own desires, and her lips opened in a sigh of surrender, welcoming the intoxication of his invading tongue.

Her body grew warm with a heat that seemed to fuse them together as he held her closer, and her hands flew up to his face, her fingertips drawing the contours of his flesh and finding an answering heat in the fire of his skin.

Words had no place. Bodies wove their own enchantment in a silent crescendo. Only the two of them were alive in the warm night, the scented garden. Thigh against thigh, mouth melding to mouth, their mingling breath was a celebration of discovery.

Feverishly Petra's hands moved to his hair, her fingers strong and seeking, weaving into its smoothness, and brushing the crisp harshness at his temples with frissons of pleasure. She could feel his hands on her back, now rough, and now in a melting caress. They moved, smoothing her ribs, then lifting to cup her small, rounded breasts. A gasp tore through her as he began to stroke the curves into a torment that made her writhe.

With a half-sob she wrenched herself away, suddenly afraid of him and of the feelings he had unleashed in her. Immediately he stepped back to stand in frozen stillness, looking down at her, his eyes shadows of dark mystery.

Her awakened desires seemed to pulsate through the night. Her senses still rocked with the realisation of his skill in understanding her needs. He had played her as if she were an instrument which he had long ago mastered. She stared up at him, her mouth tremulous, her eyes enormous.

Then she saw him smile, a white glint that moved the shadows of his face. 'You—you're really something, Petra.' His words came at last, huskily.

Yet they seemed to say nothing about his feelings.

She searched his face, looking for some clue. Was that *all?* But there was no answer in the controlled features, the smile which seemed to linger politely.

A sob rose in her throat, to be quickly stifled. His ability to govern his feelings was totally at variance with her own vulnerability. Could it be, she wondered, that his feelings were quickly aroused and died just as quickly? Was his passion only the heat of a moment? A woman, a moon, a few drinks—was that all it took? Was that all it meant?

She turned her head away. Why ask herself questions when she knew the answers? After all, she had been here before—almost!

'How well you sum it up,' she said in a cutting tone. 'A banal judgement of a hackneyed situation. You certainly have a way with words, and——'

She whirled suddenly as a clear voice said, quite close, 'Oh, *there* you are, Adam. I've been looking everywhere——'

'Why, Caroline,' Adam said blandly, after a moment.

Caroline looked enquiringly from him to Petra. 'Taking the air? You *do* look rough, Petra.' She tucked her arm into Adam's. 'Silly girl,' she went on, 'you overdid it. All those cocktails, and Adam did warn you . . . And if you're not used to it——'

'I'm perfectly all right, thank you, Caroline.' Petra resisted the desire to shout as she brushed past them. She walked on ahead. The guests in the conservatory were milling around the long table, there was the clink of crockery. Inside would be Sam . . . All that silly chatter, the game they had played, the date they were going to arrange, the sexy overtones of his talk. She couldn't stand it. Not now.

Regret, like a muddy wave, washed over her. Would she never learn? In the cold light of day Adam had no time for her. He had made that quite clear on many occasions. Even that day they had spent together had been at Venetia's instigation. He had kissed her in his room that evening—'tying up the loose ends', he had called it, then accused her of acting. But in his arms she had forgotten all that. Again, she had lowered her defences and become a slave to her body, allowing herself to be swept along by the storm of his attraction for her. Was the champagne to blame for that, too? She wished that it were.

At the bottom of the steps she hesitated, reluctant to go back inside, and she was relieved to hear Adam suggest that it might be as well to leave before the party got too hectic. Even as he spoke there was a sudden crash of crockery, followed by a loud cheer.

Caroline shuddered delicately. 'Yes, do let's go,' she murmured. 'I can't bear parties when they get out of hand.'

'How do *you* feel, Petra?' Adam said politely. In the darkness she glowered, catching the innuendo; he probably knew exactly just how she felt, she thought wretchedly.

'I'll be happy to leave.' She forced a casual note into her voice.

'Then the two of you go on to the car,' Adam said. 'I'll find our hosts and say our goodbyes.' He went up the steps into the house, a dashing figure in the swinging black cloak.

CHAPTER EIGHT

IN THE back of the car Petra sat in silence as they waited for Adam to join them. She was grateful for the darkness. Her face burned, and her head had begun to throb. The bedroom she shared with Sarah seemed like a haven, and all she wanted now was quietness and sleep. Forgetfulness.

But apparently Caroline had other ideas. 'Enjoyed yourself?' she asked creamily. 'I will say, Petra, that you do make the most of your opportunities.'

'And what is that supposed to mean?' Petra said, suddenly alert.

'Oh, come *on* . . . You know what I'm talking about. Tell me, did you say you felt like a breath of air?' When Petra didn't answer, Caroline laughed. 'You did! How transparent!'

'I really don't know what you're talking about, Caroline,' Petra said coldly. 'And in any case——'

'I'm talking about Adam kissing you, of course. He did, didn't he? It was written all over you. But a word of advice—don't assume that it meant something. Any man with a drop of red blood in his veins would have done the same, especially when it was offered up on a plate.'

Petra leaned forward, icily furious. 'Look here, Caroline,' she said quietly, 'I——'

'No!' Caroline spat out the word. '*You* look *here*. Adam and I are . . . Well, never mind. I don't have to explain to anyone, least of all to you, and——'

'You certainly don't,' Petra cut in. 'I don't want to

know. And I can't think why you feel it necessary to bring up the subject of—you and Adam. Unless,' she went on, her voice sinking thoughtfully, 'you're afraid of me. Is that it?'

'Why, of all the——'

'Oh, Caroline, how stupid of you.' What Caroline was suggesting turned a knife inside her, but she managed a laugh. 'Adam *did* kiss me, if you must know. And very pleasant it was, too.' She made herself go on. 'So what? It's a party, isn't it? So don't worry about my being so naïve as to attach any importance to it. Just relax. I'm sure you have nothing to worry about.'

In the darkness, she felt Caroline bristle with anger. 'Oh, I wasn't *worried*,' she said vehemently. 'You see, I know the score. Don't forget, I've known Adam for a long time. And *Merrill*,' she added significantly.

'I can't see that that's relevant,' Petra retorted.

'No? Now I'd say it was *very* relevant. Or don't you know?'

'Know what?'

'Why, that you look rather like Merrill, of course. Surely Venetia's mentioned it? Adam wouldn't, naturally. He never speaks of Merrill. But the resemblance must have been obvious to him.'

'You mean . . .?' All the breath seemed to have left Petra's body in a weakening rush. 'But . . . Well, I thought——' She stopped, trying to think, to remember what Sarah had told her about Merrill. 'Just what is it you're suggesting?' she whispered. 'I understood that Merrill had long, auburn hair for a start, and that——'

Caroline's laugh rippled out. 'Oh, she did. At times. She had a number of very expensive hairpieces and wigs, and her hairdresser's bill must have been astronomical. She changed her style often. And so convincingly. She could be ultra-sophisticated one week, and the complete *ingénue* the next. Quixotic wasn't the word!'

'Even so,' Petra said numbly, 'I still don't see why you have to bring up Merrill's name now.'

'Oh, Petra,' Caroline said pityingly, 'surely you're not that stupid? It's perfectly clear. Adam was misguided enough to see Merrill in *you*, because of your resemblance. And probably because you so successfully changed your image tonight—as she could. That's the reason he kissed you. He couldn't help himself.'

'Well, of all the nonsense I've ever heard——' Petra began. But she couldn't go on. She stared down at the tight silver trousers, the dark sparkle of her tunic, and a sense of utter desolation washed over her. Could Caroline be right? she wondered bleakly.

Caroline was still talking, but Petra was deafened by the tumult in her mind. She gazed unseeingly out of the car window. Maybe it did make a twisted kind of sense. It would certainly account for the way Adam had looked at her when they first met. She had seen the animosity in his eyes then; was it that he had found her likeness to his dead wife too painful to contemplate?

And there was that baffling telephone conversation with Jack Stansfield that Petra had overheard. All that she had understood then was that Adam was angry at Jack Stansfield's choice of Petra for the job.

How strange, though, that Venetia hadn't remarked upon the likeness. But then, Venetia had spoken of Merrill only once, and had been interrupted by the arrival of Adam and Caroline, so, naturally, had dropped the subject. But Caroline's explanation might throw some light on the strange glance that Venetia had given Petra on her arrival at the villa.

Oh, yes, it all made sense. It answered some of the questions that had revolved in her mind, and it explained Adam's behaviour: the kisses, half-torture, half-ecstasy; the moment of closeness before he isolated himself again. How he must have hated her for the torment of her presence. And how he must have hated himself for succumbing to a mere physical resemblance to the wife he had loved so much!

She leaned back, closing her eyes. This conversation had set the final, ugly seal on a hideous evening. Why on earth had she allowed herself to be persuaded into coming to the party? She had known all along that it would be a disaster, one way or another. But Caroline's explanation was beyond her wildest imagination.

She was silent during the drive back, longing for that moment when she would be alone again. But when she went into her bedroom she saw that Sarah was sitting up in bed, writing up her journal.

Automatically, Petra protested, pointing out the time, but Sarah said logically, 'I couldn't sleep, and I hadn't done my journal. Did you have a marvellous time, Petra?' She put aside her notebook and sat, hugging her knees under the covers. 'Tell me all about it.'

'Can't it wait until the morning?' The ache in Petra's head was a steady series of hammer blows. Then, at Sarah's disappointment, she sighed and relented. As she undressed she began to talk, describing some of the costumes, and Sarah listened, her eyes shining. 'And that's about it,' Petra concluded. 'So go to sleep now.'

'I will, in a minute. Granny told us stories.' Sarah

clasped her knees ecstatically. 'You know those two big rocks in the gorge? Well, I bet you didn't know that in old times a troubadour—that's a kind of travelling musician—fell in love with a magician's daughter. They used to meet secretly by the river. Well, the magician found out, so he turned them into those rocks. What do you think of that?'

'I'm amazed,' Petra murmured, aching for silence and darkness. 'Now, Sarah, it *is* very late——'

'But the best part is that, at full moon, they come to life and sing together!' She sighed. 'I'd love to be there. I think——'

'And *I* think,' Petra insisted quietly, resisting a desire to scream, 'that it's high time we put out the light.'

'Of course, Granny's never actually seen them, but——'

'Oh, *please*, Sarah! No more tonight. Not another word. Goodnight, now.' Petra reached out and turned off the lamp.

Caroline's words seemed to float in the air like dust motes. Petra thought of all the times that Adam's behaviour had puzzled and angered her; she remembered all the reasons and explanations she had given herself for his complexities. She had been quite wrong. The real explanation was so simple that it had never occurred to her. Well, thanks to Caroline, everything had been made crystal clear tonight.

At last she slept, and only awakened when Thomas touched her shoulder. He was carefully holding out a glass of orange juice, and she saw that he was already dressed. 'We've all been up for ages,' he said importantly. 'Granny said to let you have a lie-in. But she's going out soon. And Mummy's coming,' he added, his eyes lighting up.

Petra stifled an exclamation as she saw the time. 'That's marvellous about Mummy,' she said. 'Tell Granny I'll be down in ten minutes.'

The orange juice and a shower revived her a little, but didn't ease the blight that had settled over her. It took an effort to smile and greet Venetia cheerfully when she went down to the kitchen where Venetia was giving instructions to Monique.

'Petra, have you heard the news?' Venetia's eyes shone. 'Unity's flying out on Thursday. She's made a wonderful recovery. The children are thrilled. Oh, Patrick's gone off with Marcel, and Sarah pestered Adam so much that he took her with him to the Paiolive Woods. Caroline's still in bed. You look rather tired, dear, but you can have a quiet morning with Thomas. Enjoy the party?' she added.

'Very much,' Petra lied brightly. 'And it's great news about Unity.'

'Walk out to the car with me, will you?' Venetia picked up the navy handbag that matched her chic silk suit. 'Yes, it's wonderful news, but of course,' she went on thoughtfully, 'Unity's going to have to take things easy for a while.' She gave Petra a sidelong glance of enquiry. 'So—I wonder, would you consider staying on with us for a while longer?'

Petra swallowed. 'I—can't. I mean, I'm sorry, Venetia, but it's impossible.' The words seemed to tumble out of their own volition. Petra recovered herself, then went on more gently. 'Di—my ex-partner in the shop—wants to take a holiday, and I promised to stand in for her, so . . .' Her words trailed off lamely. It wasn't a lie, she assured herself. But Unity's recovery and Di's holiday did provide her with an unexpected, heaven-sent excuse to get away. She wondered how she could face Adam again, knowing as she now did that he had used her as a substitute for his dead wife, even as he carried on an affair with Caroline. Or so Caroline had led her to believe.

She looked away from Venetia's disappointed eyes. Don't, please don't, try to persuade me to stay, Petra implored in silent desperation. I must take this chance. And after all, the job had demanded only that she look after the children until Unity could join them. That's what Petra had undertaken to do. Just that; nothing more. So, she thought, stiffening her resolve against Venetia's crestfallen expression, she was perfectly within her rights to turn down the offer. 'I'm sorry,' she said softly, 'but I *did* promise Di . . .'

'Of course.' Venetia gave a rueful shrug. 'You must keep your word. I'm just being selfish. Don't worry, my dear, we'll manage. I understand.'

You don't, Petra thought dully, her throat solid with misery. How can you?

She glanced idly around the garden. Somehow, in this lovely place, and against her own better judgement, Adam had bewitched her. He had taken her on an emotional switchback that had hurled her from contempt and dislike up into dangerous, thrilling heights. So many times she had tried to put him out of her mind. But now she knew that to be impossible. In spite of everything, she knew that her heart overruled all her reason.

And here, under the morning sun, with the oleander stirring its pink blossom in the breeze, just trying to rationalise brought a flare of anguish, as if his power could reach out to touch her, wherever she was.

She stared hard at the gravelled drive, blinking, compressing her lips and hoping that the fall of bright hair hid her misery from Venetia. A clean break at last. That was what she was being offered. It was the only way open to her, and Unity's recovery was the best news possible.

She was conscious that Venetia was talking. '. . . miss you very much, my dear.'

Petra lifted her head, flicking back her hair. 'And I'll miss you,' she said, a little shake in her voice. 'And this lovely place . . . It's all been so—so——'

If Venetia noticed the threatening tears, she ignored them tactfully. 'We'll have to see about your travel arrangements,' she said briskly. 'You'll be flying back, of course.' She glanced at her watch. 'Must dash,' she exclaimed, and opened the car door, and Petra was grateful for her matter-of-fact tones that had defused what might have been an emotional moment.

'Ah,' Venetia said, looking beyond Petra, 'here's Thomas. No doubt he's looking for you. And there's someone else who's going to miss you.'

Petra went dully back into the house. The light chores and Thomas's never-ending questions helped to blunt the edge of her pain. But when Adam arrived back with Sarah in the early afternoon, the sight of him stirred so many contradictory feelings that Petra left abruptly and took the children down to the river.

It was during dinner that Adam spoke directly to Petra for the first time that day. 'So you're leaving us, I understand,' he said. There was a flat note of indifference in his tone, and his face was bland.

Petra caught Caroline's eyes upon her, sapphire-hard with a glint in their depths. 'Oh, well,' Caroline murmured, twisting the stem of her glass, 'when duty calls we can only obey. Do you enjoy shop work, Petra?'

Petra was saved from answering as Venetia said quickly, 'I've been thinking . . . Instead of flying, you might like to go by car with some friends of mine?' She turned to Adam. 'Tim and Brenda Stoddard—you know them, Adam—they're going to England for six weeks.' To Petra, she went on, 'Such nice people, and I'm sure you'd enjoy their company and see a little more of France en route. They'd be delighted if you would join them—especially Brenda. I was speaking to her today. Tim's a silent driver, and she would welcome a companion. Anyway, think about it, Petra.'

'I don't need to,' Petra murmured quickly. 'Thank you, Venetia. When are they leaving?'

'Wednesday. Unity arrives on Thursday, so it will work out very well.'

Petra glanced up to see Adam watching her speculatively, as if he had noticed her anxiety to get away quickly. She met his eyes steadily, then glanced away again. 'How long will you be staying, Caroline?' she asked.

Caroline lifted vague, slender hands. 'I don't know.' She looked across to Adam. 'That rather depends,' she murmured.

'Well,' Venetia said briskly, 'if we've all finished . . . Petra, why don't you play for us tonight?'

'Oh, I——' Petra stopped, not wanting to sound ungracious. Apart from supervising Sarah's piano practice, she hadn't touched the lovely old instrument since Caroline's arrival. 'Yes, all right,' she said lamely at last.

'Then I'll get the coffee.' Venetia got up.

'And I'll help you,' Caroline offered sunnily.

'Well, well,' Adam murmured, as he and Petra followed the children into the big sitting-room, 'something tells me that you simply can't wait to shake the dust of this place off your feet.'

'Does it?' Petra said indifferently, not daring to look at him. 'Why should you think that? I'm going simply because I promised Di——'

'And, of course, there's the boyfriend, isn't there? Maybe that accounts for the sudden departure. You're quite a sensation in your own way, aren't you? With the men, I mean.' His eyes narrowed to a dark glitter that captured and held her own gaze.

'What—are you talking about?' Petra whispered furiously at last. She flashed a wary glance towards the children and was reassured to see that they were noisily shaking out the pieces of a big wooden jigsaw at the other end of the room.

'Do I have to remind you of—Marcus?' Adam murmured through barely moving lips. 'How fickle of you to *have* to be reminded of the man who drove all those miles to see you . . . And then, of course, there was Sam Sheridan last night. You remember *Samson*, don't you? You never did get to fix that date with him, did you? And now it looks as if you never will.'

'Then I shall spend my entire life in futile regrets,' Petra said icily.

'Oh, I doubt that.' Adam's voice was smooth as velvet. Petra wanted to walk out, yet was unable to move.

'Well, at least *he* didn't try to kiss me and pretend——'

'Try?' A black eyebrow winged up above the dark, taunting eyes. 'I would have used the word *succeed*. A most successful kiss,' he went on, with a soft insolence that sent a shiver up her spine. 'Is it possible that you've forgotten? Is that the way it goes with you. Kiss and forget?' His attention seemed so concentrated upon her that for a moment she could only stare at him wordlessly.

At last she pulled her gaze away. 'I'd prefer not to be reminded of last night, if you don't mind. As you remarked, I was—a little——'

'Drunk? Was it only the champagne, then?'

His lazy tones boiled all the conflict of her feelings for him into a heat that made her want to strike out, smash the cruel taunt of his face into a blind anger. She wanted to scream that she was no stand-in for a woman he still loved.

'Of course it was only the champagne,' she hissed. 'So don't flatter yourself. And just for the record——' She caught her breath as his hand grasped hers in a swift, bone-crunching strength. His anger sprang to meet hers.

'Shut up,' he ground out. 'For heaven's sake, can't we——' The words were cut off as his hand dropped. In almost the same moment he reached towards the cigar box on the side table as Venetia nudged open the door with a tray, followed by Caroline carrying the coffee-pot.

Without a word Petra moved over to the piano, rubbing and flexing her tingling fingers. Anger was a live presence in the room, like a fiery arc of energy fuelled by hatred.

Adam had managed to conceal his feelings, but she sensed that beneath the long, lazy eyelids he was watching her closely. Thank heaven there were only three more days. And at least Caroline was intent upon keeping Adam occupied.

Petra sat down and without a word began to play a Litoff piece with more fire and passion than the composition demanded. She moved into a Tchaikovsky theme, and only then when she had exhausted the battle within herself was she able to give Venetia the gentle Grieg melodies she loved.

Caroline sat, her legs elegantly crossed, rustling through the pages of a fashion magazine. Adam lounged in his chair, long legs outstretched, smoking his cigar silently. Venetia hummed softly, moving one hand gently to the rhythm of the music.

Petra felt drained. Her exchange with Adam had honed her emotions to a blade of torture that mocked the pleasant music and the relaxed atmosphere of the room. Everything but her own inner turmoil seemed unreal and dreamlike.

After a while she stood up, closing the lid of the piano. 'I'm tired,' she murmured. 'I haven't caught up on last night yet. So, if you don't mind, I'll go up. Come along,' she turned to the children, 'you can finish your puzzle tomorrow.'

'Are you feeling all right, my dear?' Venetia asked, her voice concerned.

'Mmm, just tired,' Petra smiled. Venetia's solicitude was unbearable, threatening to breach the dam of her self-control. She was glad to escape from the room.

Much later she awoke and lay watching the moonlight filter through the thin curtains. The past weeks unreeled in her brain like a film, turbulent or peaceful, and always with the imprint of Adam's face, his personality, his smile, his kisses . . . Well, she told herself, the show was almost over.

It was strange to think back and realise that when she first saw this job advertised it had seemed such a good idea! A temporary escape, a breathing space in which to get herself together and plan her future. But it hadn't turned out that way at all.

She sighed, realising that sleep was further away than ever. She switched on the dim bedside-light and reached for her book. Anything was preferable to her thoughts and the longings that, despite everything, wouldn't go away.

It was then that she saw that Sarah's bed was empty. She threw on her housecoat and padded softly to the bathroom. It, too, was empty. She peeped into the room that Patrick and Thomas shared, but the two boys slept peacefully.

Obviously Sarah must be downstairs, she decided, but one glance from the landing showed Petra that the ground floor lay in darkness.

Stealthily she opened the door to Venetia's room, then, as quickly, closed it again, her heart racing. Sarah had gone. But where?

CHAPTER NINE

BACK in her own room, Petra stripped off her nightdress and threw on a tracksuit, thrusting her feet into pink trainers. There was just one more place where Sarah might be, and that was with Adam. And as Petra opened the back door she was relieved to see a glow of light behind the closed curtains of the camper.

Softly she tapped at the door, and a moment later Adam slid it back. 'Why, come right in,' he said smoothly. 'This *is* a surprise, not to mention pleasure! Such nocturnal visits rarely come——'

'Oh, for heaven's sake,' Petra snapped, dislike dripping from her voice, 'drop that . . . Where is she? Sarah?'

Adam frowned sharply, his expression suddenly alert. 'How should I know? In her bed, presumably.'

'Of course she isn't,' Petra snapped. 'Would I be here if she was? She's gone. She's nowhere in the house and——'

'Hold on. I'll get a torch. She doesn't sleepwalk, does she?' he asked over his shoulder as he opened a cupboard and groped inside.

'Not as far as I know, but I suppose it's a possibility . . . No. Wait . . . Wait a minute.' Petra was thinking furiously. 'It's full moon——'

'So?' Adam watched her curiously.

Petra raked shaking fingers through her hair. 'It's just that . . . Venetia told her some story about the two big rocks in the gorge.' Quickly she related the tale that Sarah had told.

'It's a chance,' Adam said. 'Let's go. Come on. Hurry! God forbid that she's fallen and . . . Moonlight on rocks is deceptive.'

He grabbed Petra's hand, pulling her across the garden, through the acacia grove, which was dappled black and silver. She had to take little running steps to keep up with his long, purposeful strides. When they reached the rocky bank she was out of breath.

'All right?' he asked, and when she nodded, he said, 'Follow me. Go steady, now. It won't help matters if you rick your ankle.'

Although every heartbeat was a thump of fear, Petra knew a great sense of comfort in his presence. He seemed able to take charge of things with the minimum of fuss, his broad shoulders assuming the burden of her own fearful imagination.

Carefully they wove their way over the uneven shingle and boulders towards the two big pillars, painted by the moonlight into grotesque patterns of light and shadow.

'Oh, hurry,' Petra breathed. 'If she's not there we ought to . . . Where shall we start looking? Oh, heavens, what is Unity going to think of me? And Venetia! I couldn't bear it if——'

'Shut up,' Adam hissed. Then, a moment later, his voice calm, 'She's over there.'

'Is she? I can't make out . . . Are you sure? Oh, thank heaven.' Suddenly boneless, Petra sank down, burying her head in her hands. Possessed by a flood of relief, she felt weak and insubstantial.

She wasn't aware of Adam moving quietly towards the rocks and then, just as quietly back to her, until he dropped down beside her. 'The silly child's fallen asleep,' he murmured. 'So it's all right. It's *all right,* I tell you.'

Hot tears of released tension flowed down Petra's cheeks. Agitatedly she brushed them away, not wanting Adam to see her like this. But more came, a never-ending flood, welling up, spilling over, blinding her to the beauty of the night, even to the presence of Adam beside her, until she felt his arm move across her shoulders. He drew her head on to his chest, his other hand cradling her face. His strong, steady heartbeat drummed through her relief over Sarah, but at the same time it thrummed the rhythm of the misery that had possessed her since the previous evening. And still the tears came.

'Stop it,' he said, his voice gentle. 'It's over. She's all right. Try to forget it. She's a silly girl, but I suppose it's all part of the enchantment of this place, and Sarah was always romantically inclined, imaginative.' He pushed a handkerchief into her hand. 'Now take this, and do stop crying. Otherwise we'll have the Ardèche river in flood!'

'Yes,' she gulped. 'I'm being silly. It's just that . . .'

'I know,' he said quietly. At that moment his arms seemed to hold a world of comfort and reassurance. 'I can't understand why Sarah didn't ask me to bring her down here. Or you, for that matter.'

'Maybe she wanted to be alone as part of the magic. I should have realised that it was full moon tonight . . .'

'Yes.' Adam murmured. 'The moon has a lot to answer for.'

Petra was silent. There had been a moon on the previous night. Was that what he meant? Was it his way of explaining away that scene in the Michaels' garden? It seemed years ago now, ancient history, something that had happened before Caroline's information had explained so much about Adam and his motives.

'I suppose we'd better get back,' Petra said at last.

'But—no . . . You wait here . . .' Softly she went across the beach, then crouching in the shelter of a rock she began to sing softly a few bars of a Schubert melody. Her voice was muted, smoky with misery. Sarah had come looking for magic, enchantment, unreality . . . Well, let her have it, Petra thought, her voice strengthening a little. Let her wake to the sound of music, hold on to her childish fantasies and find joy in them. She was the right age for romantic dreams . . .

Petra's voice died, and after a moment she put her hand on Sarah's arm. 'Come along,' she whispered. 'Back to bed now.'

Sarah sat up slowly, blinking. 'Did I . . .?' She stared up at Petra, her eyes wide. 'I—must have fallen asleep, I think,' she said disgustedly. 'I waited ages for the singing. Oh, I do wish I had seen them . . . But I think I heard her—the magician's daughter . . . Just for a minute.' She looked up as Adam came over. 'I don't expect you believe me, do you?' Her eyes were bright with tears.

'Oh, I believe you, all right,' he said drily. 'I heard the music, too.' He shot Petra an unreadable glance, then reached down a hand and pulled Sarah to her feet. 'I think you had better keep the story of this little escapade to yourself. Your grandmother would have a fit if she knew that you had been down here on your own. Supposing you had fallen and hurt yourself? It's easily done. And just supposing Petra hadn't woken and found your bed empty? You would be lying here until morning.'

'I'm sorry,' Sarah muttered contritely. 'I didn't think of that.'

'Well, never mind now,' Petra put in weakly. 'But *I* would have brought you if you had asked . . .' Her voice faded and died. She put out a hand to steady herself, then sat down suddenly. 'Sorry,' she said, looking up at Adam, 'but I seem . . .' She swallowed. 'It's reaction, I suppose. I——'

'Sit there,' Adam said. 'I'll take Sarah back.'

Petra nodded. 'I'll follow in a few minutes when I've got myself together.'

Dully she watched them walk away, her own words echoing through her head. It would be a long, long time before she got herself together again. How much time would she need to blunt the sharpened emotions of the last weeks? One thing was certain, she would bear the marks of her encounter with Adam for the rest of her life, because he had uncovered facets of her nature which she had never suspected could be so vivid, so overpowering.

For a while she sat quietly, her head touching her bent knees. She ought to get back to the villa; Sarah would be wondering what had happened to her. But every limb seemed limp, as if she had been drugged with some strange opiate that forbade movement.

Then she heard footsteps. Energy came back in a rush and she looked up in alarm.

'Better now?' Adam said, and dropped down beside her.

'Ye—es. I was just about to get back.' She tried to smile but her face felt stiff. 'Thank you for coming down here with me. It helped enormously to have someone to share . . . Oh, God, I was so . . .' To her utter dismay she began to cry again, weak, warm tears that threatened to drown her in misery. What on earth must he think of her? Blinking furiously, she turned away, but Adam's arm went around her as he drew her head into the hollow of his shoulder. 'You—you needn't have come back here,' she whispered in a muffled voice.

'I had to,' he said. 'I was worried about you. But it's *all right* now. Sarah went happily to bed. And that was an inspired stroke—giving her the music she came to hear. So put it behind you.' His arm tightened reassuringly, and she felt the movement of his head. Then his lips were moving over her temple, gently, soothingly. Sarah was safe. Everything was all right. With a last tiny sob she turned her face into his sweater and clung to him.

She heard his breath catch as, for a long moment, he held her perfectly still. Then with one finger he raised her chin and looked into her face. 'You're beautiful,' he whispered. 'Quite, quite beautiful. Even with tear stains . . .' His lips brushed her cheeks, slowly and sensuously. 'I can taste the salt of you . . .'

The part of her which habitually fought against his magnetism softened and finally died. She knew that this was the moment to get up and go back to the house. Before it was too late, and before the beginning of a repeat performance of other nights. She need only thank him politely for his concern for her, then close the door on him. And in three days she would be gone. After all, she knew now what lay behind his kisses, and she wasn't such a fool as to knowingly let him use her again as some temporary palliative against his ache for Merrill.

But movement seemed more impossible than before. She was a prisoner of her own longings. Could she give up this last special hour and all it might hold? All she wanted was this man, despite all the problems and complexities which threw them together, then parted them again. One last opportunity for loving. And, although he had brought her suffering, hadn't he, too, experienced heartbreak, simply by her being here, a daily agonising reminder of his wife and a happiness he had known and lost?

After Wednesday she would never see him again. The joy of his lips, the delights of his touch, the comfort he was giving her now, would all be part of the past.

With a little moan of surrender she reached up to cradle the strong jaw, then she stopped his answering groan with hungry lips.

His arms responded swiftly, pulling her towards him, uncoiling his long body until he was leaning back and they lay closely together on the moon-silvered shingle. 'God,' he breathed raggedly, 'darling . . . *darling.*'

His need touched off her own desires, fuelling the fire that blazed relentlessly as his tongue-tip explored the curl of her ear. His breath stormed and thundered through her like an exquisite hurricane. His fingers found the zipper of her blouse. Then she felt the night air whisper along her bare skin, his warm lips following in its wake . . . Travelling slowly from the delicate bones of her throat, down, down . . .

A tiny, broken cry escaped her. Half-ecstatic, half-despairing, each nerve-end clamoured and thrilled to his touch. And nothing else mattered but the passion they fed to each other.

His hands, strong and importuning, moved over her body, and she answered them with her own, thrusting his sweater up to explore the smooth, muscular back, tracing the strength and sinews that shaped the powerful design of his body while her lips brushed his chest. 'Ah, sweet . . . sweet . . .' he murmured hoarsely.

A molten heat that began somewhere in the pit of her stomach spread to suffuse her quivering body. And then, as his lips touched her breast, she cried out.

She opened her eyes to watch the movements of his dark head. She felt the slight dew of moisture on his skin. 'I want you,' he said thickly against her breast. 'I want you in any way I can take you. This is—wonderful . . . wonderful. I'm crazy for you, Petra. You know that, don't you? Let me show you, darling . . .' His fiery lips heightened the fever that surged through her. 'And love me . . . Touch me. *This* is what there is—for us . . .'

A small stone, perhaps loosened by his descent or by some small, nocturnal animal, rolled down on to the shingle an inch away from Petra's head. Just a small noise. But it sounded the knell of their lovemaking.

Petra gave a little cry of pain and wrenched herself away. 'No . . . For God's sake, no . . .' She shook her head violently, raking her hair with trembling fingers. This was all wrong! Unthinkable, in view of . . . Reason returned in excruciating agony. Her fingers fumbled nervelessly at her zipper. 'Go,' she whispered. 'Oh, please, please go . . .' She buried her face in her hands.

Adam made no movement. For a long time he did not speak, then when he did his words seared her. 'Running true to form again?'

She felt as spent as if they *had* made love. Yet she still wanted him, still burned for his touch. And, in another drab preview of the future, she guessed that she always would. But what he wanted was not *her*. He wouldn't have been making love to *her*, but to the wife who had meant so much to him. And in spite of her own torture she felt a profound pity for him and for his need which could never be assuaged. And yet, to a man of Adam's calibre, pity was a rank insult. No, she couldn't let him make love to her simply because she reminded him of someone else. It would have been too uneven, a parody . . .

'Please go,' she whispered, her voice steadying. 'This should never have happened.' She began to breathe deeply, consciously reaching for self-control as he stared at her, eyebrows drawn, his mouth tight and bitter. 'Blame it—on the magic . . . That magic that Sarah came to find. Or the moon,' she went on wildly. 'Didn't you yourself say that it has a lot to answer for?'

Slowly she got up and, walking as in a dream, she went back to the villa without turning back.

As the next days dragged by, Petra tried to tell herself that no harm had been done that night, but an inner voice argued that the real harm had been done long before, when she had first reluctantly admitted to herself that while Adam baffled and infuriated her, she was incapable of turning her back on the love she felt for him.

As she packed her bags for home she made resolute attempts to put him right out of her mind, telling herself that what she felt for Adam was probably nothing more than simple animal attraction. Hardly a noble, earth-moving emotion! And once she got home, back to the sanity of the little shop and Casterleigh, she would have a better chance of getting things into their right perspective, and seeing all this for what it was: part of the general enchantment of the place—like a holiday romance. A temporary, ephemeral thing and nothing more.

She managed to stay out of Adam's way during the last three days at the villa. The children helped, for, knowing that Petra would soon be leaving them, they clung to her, Sarah especially, wanting to be with her all the time.

Sometimes Petra, watching Adam's face across the table, and reading nothing from his expression, wondered what he was thinking. But his non-committal manner, and his readiness to be out of her company at every opportunity, convinced her that he, too, had come to his senses. At last he had realised that she was not, and never could be, the wife whom he'd loved so much.

And on Wednesday, as Tim Stoddard drove silently north, and his wife chattered vivaciously, Petra felt herself consciously letting go of the tensions that had gathered under the fluted red roof of the Villa des Roches.

When she finally thanked them and said goodbye at Southampton she found herself looking forward to getting back to her flat with the kind of anticipation that a sick person feels as each day promises a return to health.

Her careful composure sustained her during the next days. Di welcomed her back with enthusiasm, and fortunately she was too taken up with her forthcoming trip to Venice to ask too many pointed questions about Petra's last weeks. And Thea was beginning to settle down, showing a real and shrewd aptitude for the little business.

'I expect Marcus will turn up soon,' Di said, on the last evening before she left. She and Petra were having a simple meal in Petra's flat over the shop. Her dark eyes considered Petra curiously. 'I don't think he can believe that any girl could be so stupid as to turn down the chance of marriage to an Overton. But don't let him talk you round, Pet. You have a—a kind of soft streak. You can be an easy touch.'

'Don't worry,' Petra said. 'Marcus knows the

score.' She took the plates out, not wanting to mention Marcus's visit to the villa. Soft? Perhaps she had been—once. Not now, though. The experience of the past weeks had rubbed her spirit raw. And, in defence, she was concentrating on growing a callus to protect herself. It would be a long, long time before any man would pierce it.

As she set a bowl of fresh fruit salad on the table Di said, 'Well, if he comes in the shop, he'll fall for you all over again. That tan . . . And you've lost weight and look very aristocratic and—classy.' She laughed. 'You know, you haven't told me much about your job with the famous Adam.'

'It wasn't with *him*. Heaven knows, *he* didn't need a nanny.' Petra stared hard at her spoon, hoping her sudden glow didn't show on her face. 'Actually, I didn't see a lot of him. He was out on his photography jaunts . . . His mother is a darling . . .' She went on to talk about Venetia and the villa, trying to inject a note of casual enthusiasm into her voice, even as recollection stirred all the longings that she had so resolutely tried to stifle.

She was relieved when Di got up to go. 'It sounds a gorgeous place,' she murmured. 'And I do appreciate your coming back to stand in for me when you could have stayed longer. Thea's great, but she hasn't had your experience.'

Petra felt her lips move in a whimsical smile. That remark could be taken two ways.

The July days built up into a sultry, stifling heat, and two days before Di was due back bruised clouds pressed on to the roofs of Casterleigh as if trying to batten down the little town. Each blade of grass in Petra's garden was intensely green, each old brick of the wall glowed as if it still held the heat of the kiln that had fired it. Quickly Petra snipped away, cutting flowers for her pictures and jewellery before the threatening rain came.

The first large drops were falling when Thea called from the back door, 'A visitor for you,' and disappeared inside again.

It was Unity, looking fit and well and sparkling, a friendly smile on her tanned face.

'Hello, Petra,' she said gaily. 'I guess I've taken you by surprise.'

'Well, I . . . Yes, you have. Come on up.' Petra was finding it difficult to speak. Unity's unexpected appearance had thrown her thoughts into confusion. 'I—I hope you're quite better now?'

'Don't I look it?' Unity's easy informality cut through Petra's stilted manner.

'Yes, of course you do. I was about to make some coffee . . .'

'I'd love a cup!' Unity glanced round. 'What a lovely room.' Then she looked back at Petra. 'I don't blame you for being surprised to see me. I expect you thought you had seen the last of the Herralds when you left the villa.'

Petra realised that Unity was giving her time to pull herself together. 'I'll just get the cups,' she murmured, and escaped to the kitchen. Intuitively she felt that Unity's visit boded no good. Her links with the family had been cut with the last postcards she had sent to the children from Rouen on her way to Le Havre and the ferry home. She had never expected to see or hear from any of them again, except perhaps an exchange of Christmas cards with Venetia.

For a while she and Unity chatted about the children and the villa. Petra's skin prickled, waiting for the moment when Adam's name would naturally be mentioned, and staving off that time with a vivacity that rang hollow in her own ears.

But she knew that the moment must come, that sooner or later Unity would speak of Adam. Or perhaps of Adam and Caroline. Quickly she went on to talk about the shop and her tentative plans to go to New Zealand to see her father.

But when the dreaded moment came Petra didn't at first recognise it. 'My real reason for coming,' Unity said, putting down her cup with a little gesture of determination, 'is to apologise. Oh no,' she went on quickly, 'hear me out, Petra. I've had to screw up my courage to come. And heaven knows, I'm not proud of myself.' She grimaced wryly, carefully smoothing out the soft folds of the beige silk skirt over her lap. 'I'd better come straight to the point . . .' Her eyes, so much like Venetia's, were fixed seriously on Petra's face. 'No sense in hedging——'

Petra stared. 'I don't think——' she began.

'Please, Petra, listen, before my courage deserts me. I *do* owe you an apology. So does Jack Stansfield. But he thought he was acting for the best—for Adam, that is.'

Petra stood up abruptly, upsetting her empty cup. 'I see.' Her mind was busy. 'I think I can save your explanation, Unity. I know why I got the job. It was because of my resemblance to—to Merrill, wasn't it?'

It was Unity's turn to look astounded. 'You—knew?' she breathed.

'Not at first. Caroline eventually told me.' Petra saw Unity's lip curl contemptuously and went on, 'In the event, I was glad she did. The fact that I look like Merrill explained a lot—Adam's attitude to me, for a start.' Her voice faltered on his name, and she hurried on. 'At the beginning he took an instant dislike to me. He said at the time that I didn't look like the conventional nanny type, and I thought he was being a bit hypercritical. Anyway,' she went on, 'his manner was explained when Caroline spoke about Merrill.'

'I see,' Unity said quietly.

'He gave me a hard time,' Petra resumed bluntly. 'I don't think he ever believed that I had nothing to do with—whatever Jack Stansfield's motives were. And I have to say this, Unity: wasn't it a cruel thing to do? To deliberately remind him of his dead wife? And setting me up for it?'

Unity stared at her hands, her face wretched. 'We—we didn't see it that way . . . Petra, when Jack Stansfield saw you he thought that——' She shrugged, helplessly. 'Oh, it's hard to explain properly. You know,' she paused, then continued, 'when Merrill died Adam seemed to withdraw into himself. He immersed himself in work. He was always off somewhere. He seemed to—to avoid any contact with people, apart from his work, that is. You can't imagine the change in him from the brother I'd known.' She sighed. 'It's over two years since Merrill died, and he seemed to have lost interest in life. Then, when you turned up at the interview, it seemed—providential. He would see you; he'd feel *something* . . . He would be shocked into some kind of reaction. He would have to wake up to the fact that life went on, that there were girls in this world who might make him happy. That Merrill might be dead, but that there was a lot of living out there to be had. Oh, I know it sounds far-fetched, but it was just a *chance*, you see.'

'At the interview I was rather surprised at the quick decision,' Petra remarked in a hard voice.

Unity nodded. 'Jack's a close family friend, as much concerned about Adam as I was. He phoned me and sold me the idea. I went along with it. Anything, *anything* that might help Adam to—to start noticing people again.' Her voice dropped and faded.

'Well, in the circumstances, you needn't have bothered,' Petra said tightly. 'He's found Caroline.'

'I'd say *she* found *him*,' Unity murmured.

'Well, whatever,' Petra said wearily, 'he seemed to be enjoying the discovery. So don't worry about me, Unity. I appreciate your coming here, but it wasn't really necessary. You could have left things to die a natural death.'

For a moment Unity didn't speak, then she said in a low voice, 'Perhaps I might have, had it not been for Sarah's journal.'

Petra stared. 'How does that come into all this?'

'It comes into it because—Sarah's jottings were rather revealing.' Unity got up and came to stand beside Petra, her hand finding Petra's and holding it tightly. 'Sarah saw you and Adam kissing—at Moulins. She had got up for a drink of water, and she looked out of the window.' After a moment of silence, Unity resumed. 'She also wrote that you had cried in bed one evening——'

Petra's face was aflame. She pulled her hand away and went to stand by the window, absently twitching the curtains into folds.

'There were—other little things, too. At first I put it down to Sarah's imagination, but then I began to wonder . . . It was then that I realised what a rotten trick Jack and I had played on you. In all innocence. Petra, you must believe that. We had only thought to jerk Adam out of his apathy. So . . . That's why I'm apologising. The whole thing misfired. It simply didn't occur to me that you might fall in love with Adam, and——'

'But I didn't!' Petra's laugh was unnaturally high. Then she saw that Unity wasn't deceived. She sank into a chair. 'I had thought those journals would be such a good idea,' she whispered. 'But—Adam? You haven't mentioned all this to him, surely?'

'Of course not. It's entirely between us. I told Sarah that grown-up people did sometimes kiss. And there might be many reasons why you cried in bed—homesickness, for one. She could understrand that.'

Petra felt completely empty. Primly she arranged her skirt over her knees. 'So Adam doesn't know you've come to see me. Is he still in France—with Caroline?'

Unity shook her head, her long, honey-coloured hair rippling with lights. 'He left last week. He's back in London. Caroline's working in Rome. The kids are still with Venetia. I came back for a check-up, and my husband's flying in tomorrow, so we'll have a few days here together, then go back to France for the rest of the summer.'

'Give Venetia my love,' Petra said automatically.

'She spoke very highly of you. Took a great liking to you, and she's a pretty shrewd character . . .' Unity's voice died away. There seemed nothing more to say, and after a moment she stood up. 'Well, I guess I've said my piece. Petra, I can't tell you how sorry . . . I love Adam, you know,' she went on quickly. 'I just couldn't bear to see him as a shell of himself. It was a long shot, but Jack and I acted as we believed best . . . But it didn't work, did it? In France he still concentrated on his work. True, he took Caroline around a bit; he couldn't really do otherwise. But I still sensed his torment, his unhappiness beneath that maddeningly blank manner . . .'

'Well,' Petra said suddenly, 'there's only one thing to do now—try to forget it. You couldn't know how it would turn out for me. And if I had guessed at all the ramifications of taking a simple job, then I'd never have . . . I always had the feeling that Adam suspected I was part of the set-up, though. He didn't believe I hadn't known Jack Stansfield before the interview. And when I learned of my likeness to Merrill I wanted to put the thing straight, tell him I had no part in it. But,' she sighed, 'no one ever mentioned Merrill in his hearing, so I, too, kept quiet.' She ran her fingers through her hair. 'But it's time to put it behind me now. I'm going to New Zealand soon,' she said, 'maybe for good. I just don't know.' She smiled wanly. 'They say time heals all things, don't they? So perhaps it will. For me and—for Adam.'

Unity leaned forward and kissed her, her eyes shining with unshed tears. 'Thank you for not kicking me out,' she whispered. 'I know now why Venetia liked you so much.' Then she picked up her handbag and left.

CHAPTER TEN

PETRA awoke that night as the church clock struck twelve, Unity's visit still at the forefront of her mind. Time might, indeed, heal all hurts, but it wouldn't erase her feelings for Adam. The most she could hope for was that, in time, she could come to terms with what had happened.

As the echo of the last chime died away she got up to make a pot of tea, thinking dully that midnight seemed to be the hour of reckoning. It had once brought to her the absolute knowledge that she had never loved Marcus. It had been midnight when she'd discovered that Sarah was missing from her bed. Perhaps, she reflected philosophically, certain hours had a special significance to certain people.

In the kitchen she sat dismally sipping her tea. With all her heart she wished that Unity hadn't felt it necessary to come down to Casterleigh, uncovering old wounds. And what good had the visit done? Except, perhaps, it had eased Unity's conscience. But it had done nothing for Petra's peace of mind . . .

I've got to stop thinking about it, she resolved. Look forward, not back . . . New Zealand. Her father would be overjoyed to see her again, and so, too, would Moira, her stepmother. Still in her thirties, Moira was as different from Petra's own mother as it was possible to be. When her father had remarried, Petra hadn't felt that he was betraying her mother's memory in any way. And *he* hadn't tried to find temporary relief from his pain in a look-alike figure,

Petra thought bitterly. Unlike Adam . . .

Oh-h, there she went again! She dashed a hand blindly across her eyes. And yet, a silent, assertive voice insisted, could she really blame Adam? Didn't it all reveal the depth of his love for Merrill that she could still haunt him? The fact that, in certain unguarded moments, he had been unable to resist a woman who resembled Merrill was surely a measure of his devotion.

And even the fact that hatred seemed to have played some part in those wild, thrilling moments was, in a way, understandable, Petra thought. For if a man is proud, then he must loathe his own weaknesses.

Petra put her mug aside suddenly and buried her face in her hands. How fortunate Merrill had been to know such a love, a love that went on even after she was dead. And how mercilessly it showed up the true value of Petra's one-time love for Marcus!

She found a handkerchief, blew her nose and got up with a sudden clatter. The table rocked, and her mug crashed to the floor. Resignedly she fetched a dustpan and brush, swept up the pieces, parcelled them into newspaper and put them in the bin. It seemed a symbolic gesture: herself, alone here in the middle of the night, when emotions run swift and raw, clearing up the shattered fragments and disposing of them as if they had never existed.

Tomorrow, she decided, she would make enquiries about a flight to New Zealand. She could afford the trip; thanks to the sale of her share in the shop her bank balance was healthy. Perhaps she could let the flat on a short lease. Then, later, if she decided to make her home in New Zealand, Thea might be prepared to buy it from her. Things could work out very neatly.

Still intent upon this self-cleansing process, she went to the bathroom and ran a shower. The needles of water had a reviving effect, and she felt better for having made a plan, however flexible. It was something to fasten her mind on. New experience, new scenery to oust those flower-studded hills, the peach and nectarine orchards, the wild fig trees . . . Angrily she caught herself up again, wrenching her mind away from the treacherous lure of that lovely corner of France.

'And in the meantime,' she said aloud, as if she was making a solemn vow, 'I shall occupy every waking moment.' She would leave a good stock of her dried-flower work. Americans seemed to like the idea of taking home something from an English garden. With a pang she wondered what would happen to her little plot once she had left. But such morbid thoughts had no part in her future, she told herself severely.

'Is it all right if I nip out and get my hair done?' Thea asked after lunch the following day. 'I'm going to a party tonight. Why not come along?'

Just looking at Thea with her bubbly energy made Petra feel jaded. 'I'll think about it,' she smiled. 'Yes, off you go. And Thursday being what it is, I'll re-arrange the window display.'

It would be the last time she would do it, Petra thought, draping a lace collar on a stand. Di's return was imminent, and she had always appreciated Petra's flair for window-dressing.

She stood back to admire the effect, when her attention was caught by a familiar engine-note. Dismayed, she spun round and saw a white motor caravan swing into the square and slot neatly into a parking space. She stood frozen, her eyes wide with disbelief as an unmistakable figure jumped lightly down from the high driving cab.

The world seemed to hold its breath and stop. The familiar market-place outside was like an enormous painting, static and immobile. Only one man moved, lithely and with that unforgettable suggestion of purpose in every powerful line of his body. There was the same fleeting, impatient frown of uncertainty as he glanced around the square, and then . . .

Suddenly Petra could move again. She shrank back, then stepped down out of the window and on to the shop floor, fumbling her feet into the court shoes she had kicked off. She had reached the shop door and was reversing the 'Open' sign when Adam stepped under the green and gold awning.

She stared at him through the glass door, her hand still raised. But she hadn't pushed the bolt home. A brown hand firmly gripped the brass handle outside and pushed.

With a sense of impending disaster Petra stepped back as he strode into the shop. For a moment she stared at him, her mouth dry, her throat constricted. 'We—we're just closing,' she managed to whisper at last, her lips finding the words almost impossible to pronounce.

'Good,' he nodded. 'Then obviously I couldn't have timed it better.'

She turned away; the sight of him in the familiar little room with its arts and crafts and country perfumes was too much to bear. A sudden tremor shook her, shivering a cold tide through her blood. She clasped her hands tightly together in an effort to steady herself. 'Why—why have you come?' she jerked out at last.

'Why do you think?' His voice still had the power

to turn her heart over, deep, husky and infinitely disturbing. Unity's visit had been bad enough. And now—this!

'I—I really can't imagine,' she breathed.

'Well,' he said drily, 'not as a customer, that's for sure.'

'Then why? I can't think of any other reason.' She inhaled deeply, trying to quell the storm of emotion that swept through her. Her voice sounded no louder than the rustle of dead leaves. And, inside her, longing moved like a gnawing, destructive pain. She still kept her face turned away. Would she never be free of the Herralds, with their propensity for creating chaos in a life from which she demanded nothing more than to be left alone in peace?

'There are two reasons, actually,' he said tersely. 'Petra! For God's sake, look at me. I've come to see you. Isn't that obvious? I want to talk to you.' A trace of his old authority spiked his voice, and it had the effect of rallying her a little. 'Now, I'll bolt that door, then let's go through to the back—or wherever.'

'We—we'd better go up to my flat, then.' As she led him up the stairs she wished that the climb could go on for ever. He had got things wrong. There *was* nothing more to talk about. Already, there had been too much talk.

They reached her living-room and Petra sank down, exhausted for no sensible reason, passing the tip of her tongue over dry lips. The silence between them seemed thick and impenetrable. She settled back in the chair, feeling as limp as if she was stuffed with old feathers.

He stood looking down at her. The shadows below his cheekbones seemed deeper and more sombre than she remembered, his eyes more heavily lidded. She knew a fleeting wish to reach out in friendship and tell him how sorry she was to have unwittingly added to his suffering. But he probably wouldn't believe her. At last she said faintly, 'What is it you want to talk about?'

'Me. You. Us.' A faint question lit the darkness of his eyes, but his mouth seemed set into an invulnerable strength that only emphasised its sensuality. Poignantly remembering the touch of that mouth, with its violence, passion, tenderness, she gave an involuntary shudder. It didn't escape his notice, and she saw his eyes narrow suddenly, his mouth tighten.

'I don't think . . . There's nothing to say, really,' she whispered. 'Anyway, how did you find me?'

He gave a mirthless laugh. 'That was the least of my problems.' He made an impatient movement of his broad shoulders under the buff pigskin jacket. 'You had mentioned Casterleigh and the shop. And besides, Unity told——'

Petra's eyes were guarded. 'Unity told you that she came here?'

'She did,' Adam confirmed grimly. He still stood over her, hands in his pockets in that indolent stance that was part of her memories. 'We had dinner together last night with Jack Stansfield. And the whole ridiculous, stupid business was given a thorough airing.'

Petra looked down, her long lashes veiling the misery in her hazel eyes.

'I learned last night that my suspicions were correct. And I figured that Unity was well enough to face a little brotherly candour! As for Jack——' He broke off with a short laugh. 'At the very beginning, as soon as I saw you, it was pretty obvious that your likeness to

Merrill was more than mere coincidence.'

'And you thought that I was in on their—plan?' Petra said in a muffled voice.

'I did at first. Lord, how I resent interference!' He punched one hand into the palm of the other. 'And how I resented you! There's no point in denying it. To look at you hurt me. I tried to hate you. I was so furious that it wasn't difficult.'

Petra's head snapped back. 'As if I didn't know!' she sparked, a hot wave of colour coming into her face. 'You were unjust and unfair.'

He moved away abruptly and stood staring at a calendar hanging over the bureau, as if trying to engrave its design on his mind.

'On that first afternoon in France,' Petra said, 'you asked me how long I'd known Jack Stansfield. You seemed surprised when I told you that I had never seen him until the interview.'

Adam nodded. 'Yes. And I didn't believe you. I mistrusted you. I'm sorry. I was wrong.'

Petra looked up at him, remembering again those weeks when the torment of her presence must have been a daily reminder of the woman he had lost.

'I'm sorry, too,' she whispered. 'I can well understand your feelings.'

'Can you?' His eyes were sombre, but one corner of his mouth flickered in the shadow of a self-mocking smile. 'I don't think you can, Petra.' He sat down suddenly, facing her, his hands linked loosely between his knees. 'So you accepted Unity's apology?'

Petra nodded. 'She was so remorseful. I, too, was angry. But what was the point? It's all behind us now.' Heaven forbid, she thought dully, that Unity had told Adam the full gist of yesterday's conversation! 'So, you see,' she murmured, twisting her hands together, 'everything was explained and sorted out. There's no need for you to—to say any more.'

'*I* think there's *every* need,' Adam said quietly. 'And everything has not been explained. Unity doesn't know the whole story.' He was silent for a minute, as if turning words over in careful selection. Then he said in a low voice, 'I was with Merrill when she was killed.'

'I know,' Petra said quickly. 'And please . . . I know this is all very difficult for you. You don't owe me any explanations.'

'But I *do*,' he said intently, 'for the simple reason that no one except myself knows the whole story.' He leaned forward, taking one of her hands in his and chafing it gently. 'You're so cold,' he murmured wonderingly, and held it to his lips for a moment.

Petra felt that her heart was about to break. Resolutely she withdrew her hand and touched her hair.

Adam sighed and got up again and stood looking out of the window, his back towards her. 'I've come to tell you how things *really* were,' he said. 'It won't make any difference to the way you feel about me, but at least it will reassure you on certain points. You must have suffered a hell of a blow to your confidence after Caroline told you about your likeness to Merrill. I guess you thought that the only reason I wanted you was . . .' He swung round suddenly. 'I'm sorry about the way it all looked to you.'

Petra swallowed. She closed her eyes and leaned back. 'Must we go on with this? There's no point——'

'Yes, we must,' he clipped out. 'And there's every point . . . As you may know, I was driving Merrill to the airport. She—she was incapable of driving herself. She had been drinking.' His words came out in a staccato rattle, without expression. 'She had had a row with her current boyfriend and——'

'*No!*' Petra gasped involuntarily. 'Don't tell me any more. I——'

'I *must*, damn it. Can't you understand?' His voice was raw with savagery. 'Haven't you any idea at all what I'm trying to tell you? It's the truth, Petra. After all these weeks of deviousness and false impressions, I'm trying to lay it on the line! It's when people don't know the facts that they meddle, draw the wrong conclusions . . . And I'm not so insensitive that I can't see that you suffered too from interfering mean-wells.' He paused, then went on in a level tone, 'Merrill and I were in agreement on one thing—to conceal our unhappiness and keep up a pretence. Not that it was always easy. Certainly, there were times when our discretion was severely tested. But—we moved in the same circles, often working together. And at those times it seemed sensible to hide the real situation until we had got things sorted out.'

He was silent for a while, and this time Petra did not speak, sensing his need to talk at his own pace. His words had shocked her. So Caroline hadn't known the truth; nor had Venetia and Unity.

'Merrill knew that my career would last longer than hers,' Adam went on. 'I suppose I was an insurance against the time when she would have to give up modelling.'

'Oh, no,' Petra exclaimed, unable to stop herself. 'I'm sure it wasn't quite like that!' How, she asked herself in bewilderment, could any woman regard Adam as mere insurance? It wasn't credible!

He turned suddenly, his smile warm, his dark eyes alight with tenderness. 'Why, thank you, Petra,' he said softly, 'for that kind remark. But I'm sorry, you're quite wrong. It was exactly like that. Confirmation came later, along with the drinking and . . .'

'I'm—sorry,' Petra whispered simply. 'And the—the accident?'

The harsh lines settled on Adam's face again, aging him suddenly. 'Yes, that. Well, we were quarrelling—a not unusual state of affairs. I wanted Merrill to go and stay with Venetia for a while. I thought it might help . . . Quietness, relaxation, proper meals . . . Then, when she was in a better—state, we would sort things out. But Merrill didn't care much for Venetia. Nor for Ruoms. The Côte d'Azur was more to Merrill's taste. I won't go into the details, but . . .' His jaw set suddenly, and his lips hardly moved as he said so quietly that Petra had to lean forward to hear, 'She grabbed the steering wheel. It was so quick. "I'll show you that you can't control my life," she said. "I'll show you . . ." ' He stopped, closed his eyes for a moment and took a long breath. 'And that was it.'

The quiet tick of the clock was an intrusion in the silence, and any words of Petra's would have seemed an even greater intrusion. Besides, she couldn't speak. The scene that Adam had described was too tragic for Petra to contemplate fully. She saw only the horror, the ugliness, the waste. The way that people hurt each other.

'So there you have it,' Adam said at last. 'It's a little different from what you imagined, I think. Different from what you've been led to believe.'

'Adam . . . what can I say?' Petra closed her eyes against the tears that rose. 'Perhaps if Unity and Jack had known the truth——'

'What was the point? Merrill was dead,' he said

harshly. 'Why smear her name *then*? Let them remember her as the loving wife she appeared to be when other people were around. But you, at least, know the truth of it.'

'I wish you hadn't told me,' Petra murmured. Her eyes were dark with pain. He was so proud, she thought, inconsequentially. Even now . . .

'I *had* to tell you,' he said, 'so that you can believe me when I tell you my second reason for coming.' The shadows had left his face, but he was watching her guardedly. Then he came over and sat on the arm of her chair. Instantly the old magic was reborn, she was aware of him in every fibre of herself, reaching out—to him, and back to those moments once shared.

'I love you,' he said. 'Don't ask me when I woke up to that fact.' He touched her hair, his hand lingering upon its smoothness, and she felt a softness grow within her. 'That made things difficult for me, knowing what I thought I knew.' He touched the fine skin under her eyes, wiping away the dampness with gentle fingertips. 'I loved you, but hated myself for falling into what could only be a trap. The strange thing is, that the more I saw of you, the less like Merrill you seemed, until——' He stopped suddenly.

Petra turned in her chair to look up at him. 'Until when?' she whispered, still unable to take in the full impact of his words, although her heart seemed to be leaping to some crazy rhythm of its own.

'That day we spent together.' he said huskily. 'Everything was so right—until a certain moment in Jeanne's restaurant. I was going to tell you then, but you—backed off. You had a knack of suddenly slamming the door in my face.'

'It was my survival kit,' she whispered. 'You were so unpredictable——'

'And then,' he went on, 'when we got back, there was your boyfriend waiting for you.'

Petra shook her head. 'Marcus and I had broken off before I went to France——'

'Yes, so Venetia told me after you'd gone home. But at the time I was jealous as hell. He had followed you. Then the next morning I saw you with him; crouching by his chair, you looked just about as close as two people could be. And then again—that fancy-dress party, remember? Sam Sheridan? God, I thought, Merrill all over again! I fought you; I couldn't let history repeat itself. Yet, at the same time, I found you—irresistible. What the hell is a man to do in that kind of situation?'

'Oh, Adam,' she whispered, 'and what the hell is a girl to do in that kind of situation?'

He smiled down at her suddenly. 'So many mistakes,' he murmured, 'so many crossed lines, reasons why *not* . . . I should have followed my instincts.'

'You could begin now,' she murmured, her eyes alight with the love she was no longer afraid to reveal. 'I think——'

The rest of her words were lost, silenced by the turbulence of her heart as he got up, reached down and pulled her to her feet. With a great tenderness he drew her to himself as his lips sought hers. All the passion which only he could arouse surged back to meet and embrace his desire. After a long moment he held her away from him, looking deeply into her eyes. Then, with one finger, he touched her lashes. 'Still wet,' he breathed, and bent to kiss them. 'Like that night at the river . . .' he murmured. 'Do you remember, darling?' As she nodded, he said, 'I never want to see you cry again.'

'Well, it's all been rather a—lot to—take in,' she whispered.

'I know. That business about—Merrill . . . Well, I had to tell you the truth so that you can believe me now. My love is for *you*. Not for the shadow of another woman. Just you.'

She gazed up at him, her eyes shining softly. 'I *do* believe you, now that you've told me everything. But I don't think I would have before; there were too many questions, puzzles . . . Like Caroline, for example. You spent quite a bit of time with her.'

'What else could I do? She was my guest, even though she invited herself. Venetia didn't like her; I could tell. Neither did the children, and nor did you. So I kept her out of the way as much as possible.'

'And—that's all? I'm sure Caroline thought——'

He laughed, that oddly smoky sound that delighted her. 'She mistook my motives, I guess. But she's not a bad sort. She was quite philosophical when she realised that it was you I wanted, and she went off happily to Rome with that bloke she was talking to at the party.' He paused, then went on in a softly taunting voice, 'Why, Petra, darling, I do believe you were jealous!'

'You could say that,' she murmured.

'You had no cause to be. I tried to tell you that I loved you that night by the river, but——'

'You said you *wanted* me,' she reminded him gently. 'That's quite different.'

His arms tightened around her. She could feel the deep rhythm of his heart, smell the unforgettable masculine fragrance of him. 'Not for me. I love you. I *want* you; I want—*us*.'

As his voice caught on the last word, confidence in herself, in him, in a whole new future, seemed to light up the familiar room. It would never be the same again.

He tilted her head back and his mouth possessed hers again, deeply and violently, as if he could never have enough of her. His lips and hands drew her towards those waiting peaks he had shown her before, and she felt a sudden clench of ecstasy. 'Oh, darling,' he said brokenly, 'let's not bother with any more questions and answers. Nothing matters but that we've found each other.' He kissed her again, and as the world continued to rock he murmured, 'Just one thing, though . . . Remember Sarah, and her talk about being a bridesmaid?'

'Yes,' Petra whispered on an indrawn breath. 'And you told her that you had no immediate plans . . .'

'But that was then,' Adam said firmly. 'This is now.' Then, just before his lips found hers again, 'Petra, my only love, this is for ever.'